love among the shamrocks collection

Book Three

I0647894

On the
River Shannon

M. KATHERINE CLARK

ISBN-13: 978-0-9998708-5-3

Other Works by
M. Katherine Clark

The Greene and Shields Files:
    Blood is Thicker Than Water
    Once Upon a Midnight Dreary
    Old Sins Cast Long Shadows
    Tales from the Heart, Novelettes
Soundless Silence a Sherlock Holmes Novel
The Rest is Silence, an Edmond Holmes Novel – *Coming Soon*
Love Among the Shamrocks Collection:
    Under the Irish Sky
    Across the Irish Sea
    On the River Shannon
    Land Across the Sea, An Emmet O'Quinn Short
Love Among the Shamrocks Collection,
        The Next Generation:
    In Dublin Fair City
    Song of Heart's Desire
    Chasing After Moonbeams – *Coming Soon*
The Wolf's Bane Saga:
    Wolf's Bane
    Lonely Moon
    Midnight Sky
    Star Crossed
    Moon Rise
    Moon Song, a Companion
Silent Whispers, a Scottish Ghost Story
The Dragon Fire Saga
    Heart of Fire
    Will of Fire – *Coming Soon*

Prologue

"Keera!" Nessa Alexander called from down the hall. Keera O'Quinn quickly saved her progress on her unfinished novel and closed the lid of her laptop. Her roommate had just finished her last final and they were set to walk at graduation. Grinning when Ness appeared in the open doorway of their dorm room, Keera stood.

"Well?" she asked.

"Guess what just came in the mail!" Nessa pulled out a padded envelope and shook it back in forth in excitement.

"You got it?" Keera jumped up and down. "I'm so happy!"

Nessa pulled the tab at the top and the envelope made its usual tearing sound. Then Ness peered inside. Reverently pulling out the dark blue booklet, she sighed.

"It's so pretty."

"It's a passport, sweetie, not a diamond," Keera teased.

"Easy for you to say," Ness replied. "You've travelled all

over the world. I've lived exactly two places. Indianapolis and here."

"Now, the world is your oyster, so they say."

Ness's face screwed up in a cute way. "I don't like oysters."

Both women giggled and as Ness bounded over to her bunk and sat bouncing on it, Keera opened the small waist high refrigerator, pulling out a cheap bottle of sparkling wine.

"When did you get that?" Ness gasped.

"Yesterday, while you finished your neo-classical literature final. I knew we could celebrate. So," she popped the cork, filled two paper cups, and headed over to her best friend. "How did your last final go?"

"Ugh," Ness groaned. "New Age Lit is a pain in my butt. I just can't understand it all. Classics are the ones for me."

"The term is arse, Ness, it's okay to curse about New Age lit," Keera laughed. They clanked their cups together and drank.

"So good," Ness replied closing her eyes, savoring the champagne. "What about you? How did Marketing four-oh-four go?"

"Not terrible," she replied. "The presentation portion made up most of our grade and the slides were a hit, if I do say so myself."

"Was it weird finishing the project with Max?" she asked.

"Nah, we're still friends," Keera replied. "Besides our split was a mutual decision. But he may have congratulated me privately afterwards."

"Ooh, you are way too adventurous for me," Ness shook her head and sipped her drink.

"It was amazing," Keera answered. "He is really talented with certain areas."

"TMI, babe," Ness giggled.

"Oh, come on, like you aren't curious," Keera teased. "How you remained celibate all through college is amazing to me."

"Never found someone I wanted to be with."

"We'll have to find you a hot Irishman while you're visiting with me. There are so many single guys in the main cities, it's like you could have your pick!"

"I've stocked up on my Irish romance novels," Ness admitted. "I'll live in a dreamworld until my man shows up."

"Yeah, Irishmen are gentlemen in the streets and beasts between the sheets."

"Kee!" Nessa blushed red hot and looked away, then drained her champagne. "There's not enough champagne in the world to prepare me for this conversation."

"Just trust me on this, babe," she said.

"I do," Ness answered. "Speaking of Irishmen..." Ness waited until Keera refilled her cup. "Whatever happened to you and the guy you were hot and heavy with over there? I remember you wouldn't miss a single call from him the first few months then it started to taper off and you met Dylan. I'm sorry but I don't remember his name."

"Yeah," Keera looked away. "Paddy... Paddy O'Shea, he's my cousin's best friend. He's also a secret."

"What? Why?" Ness asked.

"Because my cousin Emmet would kill him if he found out."

"Is he a bad guy?"

"No," Keera defended. "He's just known as a player. We met a few years ago at a party and when I turned eighteen, we decided to give it a go. My birthday gift from him was... him." Paddy's face flashed in her mind, his easy smile, drownable eyes, and twinkling smile. But then the all-consuming mortification of the morning after and every time he called it quits when it was getting too deep, stopped her fantasy.

"I'm sorry, honey," Ness reached out and covered her hand with hers. "Did he hurt you?"

"No," Keera hurried to explain, stopping Ness from reliving her own past with her stepfather. "He was... is amazing and will always be the man I love but..." Keera shook her head and forced the sad thoughts aside. "I fully intend on hooking up with him while I'm home."

Ness smiled slightly and Keera knew better than to force happiness with her best friend. Ness knew her better than anyone, save her mother and cousin, Emmet. Even having only met their first day on campus two years ago, Keera counted her freckly faced, redheaded, American friend as a sister.

"Listen, in two weeks, we fly to Ireland and if I can't get you a boyfriend by the time of my cousin Sean's wedding in a month, then I'm a crappy best friend."

Ness' smile bloomed. "Deal," she raised her cup and tapped it against Keera's then drank.

But no matter how hard she tried, she couldn't get Paddy's face out of her head all evening, all week, and the long month back in County Clare.

Perhaps she could sneak out and see him while everyone was at Sheehan's pub in Killarney. It would be the first time in two years. It had to be perfect.

Chapter One

Three weeks later

"Men are gobshites honey, I'm sorry," Keera stated, wrapping her friend in her arms.

"Oh, tanks very much," Emmet grumbled.

"Cheers," Paddy said from behind the counter. Keera resisted looking over at him. It was the first time she had seen him and even though they had been texting all week, she had yet to hold him, smell his musky cologne, or feel his silky hair beneath her fingertips. But her cousin Emmet was right there and if she looked over at his best friend, he would know something was up.

"Emmet told me what happened," Keera went on. "I can't believe that arsehole!"

"Kee, it's okay," Ness soothed.

"No, it's not," Keera said, her anger over the situation with her cousin Sean taking precedence. "But listen, I'll pack you some things when I get back. We'll go down to Dublin and get us a couple hot barmen. We'll flirt the night away. Oh, and we'll have Emmet to make sure no guy gets too close."

She risked a glance at Paddy then, only to see him looking down at the computer, his jaw was set and his eyes hard.

"Oh?" Emmet asked drawing her attention. "And what if I want to leave early to have me own fun?"

Keera waved him off. "We all know you've been celibate since Chloe."

Emmet stared at her and she tried not to laugh at the shock and horror on his face. "Right, 'cause *that's* normal."

Ness laughed and Keera turned back to her best friend. "Anyway, stay here for a little, go see the Ring and Emmet will look after you. Get Sean out of your head."

Ness nodded and after a quick hug, Keera headed to the door. She could feel Paddy's eyes on her. Hearing the elevator ding, she paused just inside the vestibule and looked back. Ness and Emmet were in the elevator and the doors were closing. Paddy was watching her, his light brown eyes suggestive and her body burned. Peeking back in, she moved her head indicating outside and he nodded.

It had been far too long. Too long without Keera. When he saw her breeze into the lobby of the hotel he worked in as carefree as she did everything, Paddy nearly gave the whole thing away. Wanting to jump over the counter, which would have been a feat in itself as the counter was well over four feet tall, race to her and kiss her senseless, Paddy tampered his initial reaction. Emmet, his best friend and sometimes boss at the car dealer, was standing right beside the young woman Paddy was helping get two rooms for the night. Initially, when the striking young woman came in asking for two rooms and dropping Emmet's name, Paddy wanted to tease. They both brought conquests back to the hotel, it was the best place since no one wanted to give out addresses to a potential one-night stand. But when he saw her tear-lined, red rimmed eyes, he refrained and was glad he did. Apparently, the girl had been hurt. Then in she walked; looking gorgeous and sexy as hell.

Once all the fluff was through and Keera turned away from them all, Paddy waited to call to her. He needed to make sure no one knew about them and since Emmet used to work at the Plaza Hotel, he still had friends. Seeing her wait inside the vestibule, made his palms sweaty and his blood pressure skyrocket. Her little nod to outside, made his heart jump. Cursing his reaction, he reminded himself he was a confirmed bachelor like his Uncle Tully, even if thirty-three years separated them.

But it was Keera O'Quinn.

He felt differently about her, always had and that thought scared him.

Asking his coworker to take over the front desk, he stepped out the employee's entrance, and saw Keera waiting in the shadows.

"Gobshites? Really, Kee?" he teased, and it felt good to be back to their old rhythm. The sheepish grin that spread over her lips lit her eyes and made his chest ache.

"Why not? It's true. Prove me wrong," she stepped closer to him.

In an instant, he had her pinned to the wall with his body and his lips on hers. Growling, he pushed his tongue into her mouth to duel with hers. She rubbed her hands up and down his chest, growing bolder than ever before. He pulled back with a curse.

"Damn," he said. "I've missed you, Keera."

"Why didn't you come to Blarney Castle earlier?" she asked in-between kisses.

"I had to work, love," he replied. "I've been here since noon."

"Too bad," she moved to his neck and he sucked on the tender spot just behind her ear. Her breath shuddered. "I had the perfect spot picked out."

"To do what?" he coaxed.

"To show you how much I've missed you."

He groaned and instantly there were too many layers between them. He pulled off his suit jacket and her coat.

"We don't have much time, so you're going to have to make it quick," she breathed, helping unbutton his shirt.

"We have all the time in the world."

"I have a beer and a cig waiting for me."

"Since when did you pick smoking back up?" Paddy asked.

"Since there's a right wetser of a man waiting for me."

An unfamiliar emotion bubbled to the surface and before he could suppress it, he pulled away and looked her in the eye. The ugly truth sunk in. She was only there for a quick hookup. His stomach plummeted and his heart slowed. He meant nothing to her.

"So what? I'm just another piece of fun for you?" he demanded. She looked at him then burst out laughing. Pulling away from the wall, he began buttoning up his shirt and tucking it into his pants.

"Do I need to remind you about our first time? *My* first time? You left in the morning without so much as a goodbye."

"That was then," he justified grabbing his jacket off a couple pallets used by the kitchen staff.

"And now is different?" She questioned. He looked back at her; her flushed cheeks, red lips, and mussed hair. She was so beautiful and yet the jealousy stung, giving their reunion an agonizing end. "You were very clear you weren't looking for anything and no commitment was made before I left," she reminded him.

"What do you expect from me? You come here; I haven't seen you in two years. I read your signals. I come out here and you only want me to hurry up so you can go back to another man waiting for you? What do you expect me to feel?"

"There's nothing permanent with us, Paddy," she replied. "You don't want anything more. Why would you care if I have another guy or two waiting for me?"

"Dammit, Keera, you aren't supposed to be like that."

"Like what?" she demanded.

"Like all the others. I thought you were different. Special. And here you are, just like everyone else."

"You were the one who told me you didn't want a relationship! You never said anything in all the texts, calls, hell even emails, that you wanted anything more."

"I don't."

"Then forgive me if I don't quite understand what you're trying to say. We have never had a relationship. It's a good time between two people who are attracted to each other. That's it, or do you not remember your words to me before I left for America?" She grabbed her handbag and headed down the alley.

"Keera," he called but she didn't respond, instead she kept walking. "Keera."

"What, Paddy?" she whirled around.

"I..." he couldn't say the words. They were on his tongue, but he couldn't breathe them to life.

She licked her lips and he saw the telltale shimmer in her eyes. "That's what I thought." Without another word, she turned back down the alley and out of sight.

After a moment, Paddy raced after her only to see her joining a group of men out front of Sheehan's. One of them greeted her with a smack on the arse and a beer, another offered her a cigarette. Paddy growled. But Keera laughed and took the man's cigarette with a suggestive wink. The one who gave her a beer, leaned in and his lips moved near her ear, but Paddy couldn't hear nor see what he was saying. But Keera grinned and after a puff, she took the man's hand and they walked around the side of the pub to another darkened alley.

Paddy knew exactly what was going to happen and he took two steps forward to stop it but froze. They had fun, always did. But when she told him over the phone, she wanted to see other people while in America, his image of the future with her in it, shattered. He remembered that day. His Uncle Tully pulling him back from the figurative edge. Pulling out his phone again, he dialed quickly.

"Paddy, my boy," his uncle's familiar voice rang over the phone. "How are ya?"

"She's gone, Uncle Tully. I had her in my grasp and I screwed up... again. I..."

"Tell me what happened, lad," his familiar smooth baritone grounding him. Tully was the only one he had ever told. When Paddy and Keera were together for the first time, her first time, he had held her to him as she slept and after kissing her temple, had said three words to her he never told another partner.

I love you.

And it had scared the shite out of him.

Chapter Two

Fifteen Months Later

Keera stared down at the pregnancy test as her hand shook. The double lines blurred as she swayed. How could she be pregnant? She took every precaution. She couldn't be. It had to be a false positive. There was no possible way... but there was... Her on-again-off-again boyfriend; Patrick O'Flannery and she had been more on than off in recent months, even if they had broken up for good a month ago. But her missed cycle and the two lines on the stick, clearly showed he had left something with her.

She screeched when someone knocked on the door.

"Sweetheart, are you all right?" her mother called.

"Fine, ma," she answered through the closed door, her voice only wavering slightly.

"All right, darling, well, hurry up. Your Aunt Dee just called. We need to head over. Emmet has something to share with us all."

"I'm really not feeling well, ma. Can you go and tell me what it is?"

"Oh sweetie, I'm sorry was it something you ate?"

"No," then she thought better of it. "Maybe," she fibbed. "I don't know."

"Well, you know I would honey but Emmet need our support right now. It might be about the hearing for his son. Come on, maybe some fresh air will do you good."

Keera knew she was right, but she couldn't bear going to see her family especially not the ferry ride. The mere thought of it made her want to vomit up her breakfast. But the drive alone with her mom was what she didn't want. Her mother was so perceptive, she would know something was wrong and she just couldn't bring herself to tell her mom who, twenty-three years ago, had been in that very bathroom vomiting and crying over a positive pregnancy test. She just couldn't tell her. Siobhan had sacrificed so much so Keera wouldn't end up like her but, what happened? Some stupid boy, that's what, and not the boy she wanted either.

Shaking her head, she hadn't seen Paddy since that night in Killarney where she first met Patrick O'Flannery. She didn't want to admit she missed him. She didn't want to admit she still had dreams of laying with him in Killarney Park on a beautifully warm day, having a picnic and making love under the shade of a tree.

He meant something to her, she would be the first one to admit it, but he had never come after her. He was a stubborn bastard, that much was clear, but she had hoped... no, it wasn't going to happen, but she hoped he would come back to her.

Splashing cold water on her face, she took several deep breaths and forced herself to smile. Opening the door, she saw her mom down the hall scurrying around in the kitchen.

"Ma? What are you doing?" she asked.

Her mom turned to her. "Oh, honey, you look so pale. Are you sure you're all right?"

"I'm fine," she answered quickly. "What's with the take-aways?"

"Well, I figured whatever you got into should be in last night's dinner so I'm tossing it out."

"No, ma, it's not from dinner last night."

"You don't know, honey, better safe than sorry."

Safe... she thought was being safe. Apparently not.

"Ma, it's not the food," she said.

"Was it the chips?" she asked, not listening and still moving around the kitchen.

"Ma, no."

"What about the beans from yesterday's breakfast? It could have been them. They smell off to me."

"I'm pregnant," Keera finally said.

There was a crash behind the open refrigerator door, then silence. Finally, Siobhan walked out into Keera's view. Her face was pale and blank.

"What did you say, love?" she finally asked.

"I'm pregnant, ma. I'm so sorry." Keera finally burst into tears.

Siobhan raced to her daughter and grabbed her tightly in her arms. Keera cried harder into her mother's chest. Throughout her tears, her mother held her close, speaking softly but letting her cry. When Keera finally calmed enough, she pulled slightly away but Siobhan led her over to the couch.

Sitting together after Siobhan grabbed some tissues, Keera dried her eyes and picked at the remaining tissues. Her mother softly stroked her back, giving her a chance to calm down.

"I'm sorry, ma," she finally said. "I took every precaution but somehow..."

"Nothing is one hundred percent, sweetie," her mom replied. "Which test did you do?"

"I got one from a place in Ennis. I didn't want anyone to know. I just took it."

"How late are you?"

"I missed last month but I didn't think anything of it then. I was supposed to start a week ago, that's when I realized I hadn't..."

"Is it Paddy's?" she asked gently.

Keera's eyes shot up to her mom. She and Paddy had agreed not to tell anyone for fear of her cousins' reactions.

"Sweetie, I wasn't born yesterday, I've been there. I've also seen the looks between you both. I'm guessing you've been together since before you went to America.

"We... we were but... it's been a while and I'm with Patrick O'Flannery now... on and off."

"Does he know?" she asked. Keera shook her head.

"We broke up... for good this time, last month."

"And there's no one else?"

Keera shook her head again. "I'm so sorry, ma. I know how much you've sacrificed for me trying to get me to school and a good job. I'm so sorry."

"Sweetie, my one concern is *you*. Yes, it's not ideal but, honey, I love you. Now, we need to set a time to meet with a doctor. You got this and I will be with you every step of the way."

"I don't know, ma. I don't think I can do this. I'm not like you. I'm not as strong as you were."

"You are, and I wasn't very strong, sweetie. Your gran and grandad helped me so much. I'll never forget how they took care of me. You'll always have me, sweetie. And I'm going to tell you what my mother told me, all right? She said *rejoice, that's a new life you're bringing into the world. Not everyone gets to feel their baby grow inside them, some women will never feel the sheer love of being able to hold your newborn in your arms.* Some women try and try only for disappointment. You were chosen to bring this life into the world. You get to enjoy those moments. Celebrate it. It's nothing to be ashamed of, it's something to be so grateful for."

"You'll help me?" she begged.

"Whenever and however you need me, love, always," Siobhan smiled and tucked a strand of hair behind her ear. "I do think you need to tell Patrick. He deserves to know. He is the father."

Keera violently shook her head. "No, I can't. He won't want the baby. I know he won't."

"You don't know that until you ask."

"I can't marry him."

"No one said anything about marriage, love. But he has a right to know."

"Did you... did you tell the man who fathered me?" Keera asked.

"Yes, I did," she replied. "But my experience isn't the same as yours could be."

"He didn't want me, did he?"

"That's not true, love," she sighed. "You've never asked about your da' before."

"I've not been pregnant before..."

"Touché," she answered. "He was not in a position where he could do anything about it. And if I told anyone else, his life would be ruined. I loved him. I couldn't tell."

"He was married, wasn't he?" Keera asked.

Siobhan took a deep breath and nodded. "My professor. But he wasn't terrible, honey. He was concerned and he was there for me when he could be."

"But he didn't attempt to be in my life at all."

"He couldn't," Siobhan shook her head.

"Why not? Didn't he want to meet me? At all?"

"Yes, of course he did," Siobhan replied. "But... he couldn't. I wouldn't let him. He had so much to lose."

"And what about me? I've lived my entire life without my father."

"I know," she looked down.

"Do you still talk to him?" Keera asked.

"No," Siobhan revealed. "I haven't since you turned eighteen and I asked him to come to your party. He couldn't or wouldn't. And that was it. But enough about that. I know it's not ideal, but Deirdre was very anxious that we get there before noon." She kissed her daughter's forehead and cupped her face. "Go and get dressed. We'll swing by my doctor's office on the way back. He is very nice, and I'll talk to them. See about getting you in today. Let him do a test again and get you on some prenatal vitamins."

Keera huffed a sigh and agreed, hurrying down the hallway to her room.

Paddy stared at Emmet for a long minute.

"Are you taking a piss? First, you tell me you're marrying this lash then you tell me I'm going to have to work with *Tom Callahan*? You swore to castrate anyone who spoke his name and now you're wanting him to work here?"

"He needs a job," Emmet explained. "And I never said I'd

castrate anyone. I was langered if I did. But aye, he's going to work here. Today is his first day and I need you to train him."

"Train him? Go way outta that."

"Paddy, I need you. You're me best salesman. Please."

"Ah, hell, flattery will get you everywhere, O'Quinn. Fine. But you owe me a pint."

"Make it two," Emmet agreed and slapped him on the shoulder. "Cheers, mate."

"Lay off," Paddy replied. "What time is he going to be here?"

"I told him ten, so any minute," Emmet stated.

"Boss," another salesman knocked on Emmet's open door. "Tom Callahan is here. Says he has a meeting with you?" the man's eyes were wide, and Paddy didn't miss how he shielded his lower region with his hand when he said the name.

"Aye, cheers, thank you. Have him come in," Emmet replied then turned to Paddy. "Thank you, Paddy. I owe you one."

Nodding once, they both looked to the door when Tom knocked.

"Tom! Good to see ya," Emmet pulled him into an embrace and Paddy thought for sure the cameras would descend. He had to be on some crazy show. There was no way Emmet O'Quinn and Tom Callahan were talking again, let alone embracing.

"Thanks for having me," Tom replied and looked over at Paddy.

"You remember Paddy O'Shea, two years behind us in Primary?" Emmet reintroduced.

"Yeah of course," Tom answered and stuck out a hand for him to shake. Paddy shook himself out of his stupor and took the hand.

"Good to see you again, Tom," Paddy said. "Welcome."

"Cheers, thanks," Tom replied.

"Paddy will be your trainer; any questions just ask."

"Great, thanks for agreeing to helping me."

"No worries, you'll learn quickly. Ehm, let's start with the breakroom." Paddy offered to have Tom go ahead of him and then glanced back at Emmet. His friend had a smile on his face that hadn't left his lips since he first met Mara McGrath. Paddy rolled his eyes and joined Tom in the hall.

Chapter Three

One Week Later

Keera's hand shook as she and Siobhan waited in the hospital. Seeing Emmet shot on the steps of the courthouse would stay with her for the rest of her life. Then, for Ness to go into labor... she shook her head to clear it. Her mom brought her some herbal tea and smiled slightly.

"They'll both be fine, love," she said as she sat beside her. "Ness is young and strong. She'll have that precious baby in her arms in no time. Don't you worry."

"I'm not," she said, though to be honest, she was. In a few short months she could be experiencing the same thing. Monday she and her mom had stopped in at the local doctor who took a urine sample but didn't have the lab needed and had to send it out. It would take two to three days for the results and that's if they moved quickly; which knowing country doctors wouldn't happen. Keera almost wished they had gone to Dublin to have the test done there. The old doctor assured her, store bought pregnancy tests weren't always accurate. But she knew in her heart she was. Blowing on the hot tea, she sipped it and hummed.

"Thanks, ma," she said.

"You're welcome, sweetie. Any news on Emmet?"

"Nothing yet," she breathed. "To see him like that. I—"

"I know," her mom said but the sound of her voice cracking made Keera look over at her.

"He'll be okay, ma," she said.

Siobhan nodded and patted her cheek. Ever since before Keera was born, her mom was close to all her nephews. When their mother died, Siobhan took on the mantle but that was after Keera was born and not easy for her.

Orin and Deirdre, Emmet's father and stepmother, walked down the hall to them and Siobhan and Keera stood.

"Anything?" Siobhan asked.

"He's still in surgery," Orin stated but Keera saw the tightness around her uncle's eyes and mouth.

Deirdre patted her eyes dry. "We just came from Sean's and Ness's room. Her contractions are about five minutes apart and she's dilated about five centimeters. They're going to be a while."

"How's Sean holding up?" Innis asked walking up to them, a cup of cappuccino in his hand.

"He's not doing great," Deirdre revealed. "He's worried but not showing it to Ness. And he's worried about his brother."

"I'll go talk to him," Innis offered, and Orin took him

down the hall toward the maternity ward.

Deirdre sat with them and allowed Siobhan to take her hand. Leaning her head back against the wall, she sighed.

"Please tell me some good news, something to get my mind off my boy fighting for his life," Deirdre begged.

Siobhan looked over at Keera but said nothing. "How's Sinéad?" Siobhan asked after Deirdre's daughter.

"She's scared, but she went home with Rachel and Trish. She was worn out from crying, poor lamb."

"It's been five hours, surely they know something by now," Keera demanded and stood.

"Cabhan said it could take a long time, honey," Deirdre said.

"But they should tell us something," she began to pace.

"Keera," her mom cautioned. "Calm down, honey. Stress is not good for the—" she stopped herself when Keera turned wide eyes on her mom.

"Baby?" Deirdre intuitively finished. She jumped up and rushed to Keera. "Sweetie, are you pregnant?"

"I—"

"Oh honey, I'm so happy!" Deirdre pulled her into a bone-breaking hug. "When are you due?"

"I—"

Someone cleared their throat behind them, and Deirdre pulled away and looked at who had arrived. When Keera locked eyes with Paddy O'Shea, her stomach dropped. Paddy looked damn good, dressed to the nines. He wore a suit, different from his uniform at the Plaza Hotel. His dark auburn almost brown hair was brushed and soft, his jaw was covered in a week's worth of stubble but his light brown eyes stared holes through her.

He said nothing but Keera knew he had heard her aunt.

"Paddy," her mother said with a smile, standing and heading over to him. "It's good to see you again."

"And you, Ms. O'Quinn," he said finally pulling his eyes from Keera to greet her. "I heard about Emmet. I wanted to check on him."

"He's still in surgery, Paddy. Thank you, love," Deirdre explained.

"Do they have any idea what happened?" Paddy asked, not looking at her.

"He was shot twice in the chest by Mara's ex-boyfriend. He fell onto the steps holding Trevor, his son. The little one is all right, but Emmet lost a lot of blood and they're worried about the location of the bullets. One is at his sternum and the other is... directly below his heart. They said it's a miracle it didn't go right through it. He's in surgery but the outlook is... grim," Deirdre explained, tears again gathering in the corners of her eyes.

"Did they catch this guy?" Paddy asked.

"Yes," Deirdre answered. "He's in custody but no one has seen Mara since it happened."

Keera's ears were ringing and as much as she tried to focus on the rest of the conversation, she stared at Paddy. Watching him, waiting for him to look at her, and when it didn't happen, she willed it but still it didn't happen.

Just once, she would have loved for him to look at her the way he had before. Just once. It would help her get through the next few years, if he only looked at her.

While she was in America, his weekly calls had been a lifeline in a new place and when they were able to Skype, it was even better but after her first year, she started taking less and less of his calls. She had her own friends and she and Ness were hanging out more and more. When she did answer, their conversation fell into an easy rhythm, but she wanted more. She wanted exciting. She wanted fun, like Paddy used to be.

When she returned from America, they continued their secret and she loved it, but as soon as he expected her to have saved herself for him when he hadn't done the same, she was done. She was tired of chauvinistic society. The man could do whatever he wanted with no consequences, but a woman slept with two or three men, she was a slut.

She and Paddy hadn't talked since that night fifteen months ago and looking at him, she realized how sorry she was for that. Patrick O'Flannery was dangerous, fun, and interesting. But he was not her ever after. Looking at Paddy O'Shea, in all his *GQ* model glory, she knew she wanted him and maybe it wasn't too late. But then she felt a fluttering in her stomach, butterflies she thought, or maybe... Paddy would never want to raise another man's child.

Is it possible for your heart to stop beating for a solid ten seconds? Paddy wondered. *If not, thank god I'm in a hospital.*

When he had heard Keera's voice, he instinctually followed the sound but as he stood there, forcing himself to listen to Deirdre tell him what happened to his dearest friend, he could not stop his thoughts.

Keera was pregnant.

For a split second he hoped it was his, but then realization overcame, and he knew it couldn't be. Then anger had surfaced, and he suppressed it. If he gave in and looked at her, he wouldn't have a chance and he would be back to the sniveling, whipped puppy she seemed to enjoy. But god help him, he wanted to look at her, he wanted to see she wasn't all right with this, with the baby, with the way things were left between them.

But he would never feel that way again. He wouldn't allow any woman to make him feel less than he was.

"The doctors are trying to be hopeful but it's the one that

nicked his lung they worry about. But at least it wasn't his heart," Deirdre finished.

Paddy nodded once. "Well, I'm glad he's going to be all right. We've closed up the dealership for the day, but I wanted to check on him."

"I'm sure he'll be glad you did," Siobhan said.

Paddy thanked her and then looked down. "I should go."

"No need, love," Deirdre replied. "It's good to see you, Paddy. Stay."

"Thank you, Mrs. O'Quinn, but I can't," he answered. He felt Keera's eyes on him the whole time and if he didn't get out of there quickly, he wasn't sure he had the will to leave again. He had prided himself on moving on with his life, putting Keera behind him, even if he wasn't fooling anyone. He hadn't been with anyone in the fifteen months they had been apart.

One glance... She looked so scared, all he wanted to do was pull her into him and keep her safe, fight all her battles.

Dear god in heaven, I still love her.

Chapter

Four

Watching Paddy walk away was even more difficult than Keera expected. With a glance at her mom, Keera never expected her to nod and mouth, *go.*

Hurrying out the main entrance, she saw his retreating figure and called out to him. "Paddy!" He stopped midstride but didn't turn until she was directly behind him. "Paddy," she said again. Finally, he turned to her. "It's good to see you."

"You too, it's been a while," he said.

"I texted you about a month ago, did you get it?" she asked.

"I did," he answered. "I was... busy."

"Yeah, I get it."

"Congratulations, by the way," he said pointedly looking at her stomach. "I'm sure the father is very happy."

"I haven't told him," she admitted. "I'm still waiting on confirmation from Dublin. The doctor here didn't have the right equipment to give me a clear answer."

"Then how do you know?"

"I took a test at home," she replied. "I'm so sorry how things were left between us. I was angry at you but mostly at myself. Paddy, I—" She cleared her throat and looked down. "Today showed me how short life can be and I don't want another second to go by without you by my side. Please forgive me and please give me another chance. I care about you so much. I... I know I have no right, considering," for the first time, she placed a hand on her lower abdomen. "But maybe we can start over?" She felt sick. Putting herself out there was never easy, but putting it all on the line with the man she loved? Even harder.

Paddy said nothing for a while. Still shielding that part of him, she wanted so badly.

"Keera," he took a deep breath but with one step forward, he placed his hand over hers on her stomach and looked up into her eyes. She held her breath. "I have always wanted to be with you. But I have to ask... are you sure?"

Keera nodded as a tear slid down her cheek. "I'm sorry."

"Hey, enough of that," he stepped closer to her and wrapped her in his arms. "I'm sorry, too. We both expected different things from each other. But now, let's face it together, aye?"

She nodded. "I'm scared, Paddy."

"It'll be all right," he pulled her to him and kissed her hair.

"I was hoping you would see how sincere I am, and it would be easy for us. I didn't expect it to be wonderfully easy."

"I could never deny you anything, you know that."

"I do. I'm so tired," she mumbled, and it was true, at that moment it seemed like everything that had happened that week came crashing in on her and she was so very tired.

"Come back to my place. You can sleep."

"Only sleep?" she questioned a hopeful gleam in her voice.

"Yes," he stated. She pulled back and looked up at him.

"Is this how it will be?" she asked. "You won't touch me?"

"Not when you're too tired," he answered.

"If I'm pregnant, I might be tired more often."

"That's all right. I'm older now, may not be able to keep up with you," he winked.

She laughed but took his hand in hers.

"Then take me to your flat, Paddy."

"When everything is better and Emmet is out of the hospital, let's go somewhere just the two of us. I want to actually go out on the town with you and not sneak around like we had to at Sean's rehearsal dinner with Trish."

"That'd be nice," she sighed as she got into his car. "But there's a small problem."

"What's that?"

"We have to tell my cousins about us."

He made a groaning sound and put his forehead on the steering wheel.

"Can we tell them while we're away?" he asked. "The farther I am from them, the less likely they'll take my bollocks."

Keera giggled but took one hand in hers. "Don't worry, my cousins won't hurt me, and I'll stand between you."

"So thoughtful," he grumbled but his smile was broad.

"Come on. I'm sure you're starving. I'll make you a BLT before you lie down."

"Ugh you would use bacon against me," she teased as he pulled out of the parking spot and onto the main road.

Paddy sat with Keera and Siobhan at the doctor's office waiting for the old man to join them with the results. Emmet was still unconscious for the third day in a row, but Keera got the call while they were driving back to her aunt's and uncle's the afternoon before.

The only noise in the room was the tick tock of the clock above them and it drove Paddy crazy. He had changed from leaning forward with his elbows on his knees, to leaning back with his hands on his thighs, to allowing his knee to bounce uncontrollably.

Last night, he had driven her back to his flat, tucked her into his bed and left to make her favorite BLT. When he had returned to his room, she was fast asleep. Staring into her face for a long moment, he remembered how much of an arse he was to her that first time and yet she still accepted him back again and again until the last time.

He set the plate of food and a water for her on the nightstand. *Knowing* he should leave and *actually* going were two separate things. He wanted nothing more than to slip between the sheets and hold her. She looked so scared earlier at the hospital, he wanted to take all of her fears away.

Instead of taking the advantage, a new concept for him, since he normally took even the smallest grain of a woman giving in and used it to his advantage, he took a seat in the chair he had in the corner for reading and opened his book. Hating that he was at the age he needed reading glasses, he took them out of their secret place behind the lamp. He glanced over to Keera, still asleep, and slipped them on. No woman had ever seen him wear reading glasses and honestly no woman knew he was a book worm, two things he kept very close to his chest. It's not as if a bibliophile wearing reading glasses fit the bad boy persona he exuded.

Soon the story of the latest thriller captivated him, drawing him in, he didn't hear the sheets rustle until he heard her soft giggle. Looking up, over his glasses he saw her staring at him.

Quickly removing the eyewear and placing a bookmark in the book, he looked at her sheepishly. She opened her mouth to say something, but he beat her to it.

"Say one word about my age and I'll tickle you mercilessly and remember, I know all your spots."

She closed her mouth quickly but then started giggling again. He set the book aside and stood slowly. She still giggled as she stared at him holding the sheet up to her mouth as if a shield. He shook his head in feigned disapproval but quickly pounced and tickled her. She screeched and tried to push him away. He didn't let up and dodged her flailing arms and legs.

"Stop," she screeched.

"Say you're sorry," he taunted.

"I didn't say anything!"

"You had a look," he answered, letting up a little just in case the baby would be hurt.

She looked up at him and grinned. "I was just curious... how did you know I had a professor fantasy?"

"Oh, you asked for it," he breathed and doubled his efforts.

Shrieking, she fought him off, but he was easily able to dodge her swings, laughing as he did. Finally, he took pity on her and slowly let up. She fell back onto the bed breathless but soon her giggling came back as she looked up at him straddling her.

But he said and did nothing as she stroked his hair. For a moment, he wondered if she'd make some quip about his two grey hairs. He almost hoped she mentioned his name and the words *Silver Fox* in the same sentence, but when she sighed and a soft smile lit her lips, his breath nearly froze in his lungs.

"I've missed you," she whispered.

His heart lightened for the first time in fifteen months. Slowly, he leaned down. When he hesitated, another first for him, she raised her head and kissed him. What started as an innocent game soon turned into a seduction. Before he could not stop either of them, Paddy pulled away and stood from the bed.

"What?" she gasped.

"You're tired and I don't want you to think I expect that. You are welcome to stay here for however long you need but it won't be in exchange for sex."

She looked at him for a long moment before she nodded. Sex had gotten her into this predicament. To hear he didn't expect that, made something, long dormant inside her heart, spring to life.

"Thank you," she said. Then to lighten the mood and her own thoughts, "I do like the glasses though. How long have you had them?"

"A little over a year," he admitted. "They make me feel old."

"They make you look hot," she said. "And since when do you read?"

He looked down and away, an embarrassed look on his face, then shrugged. "I've always loved reading. I've been a pretty avid reader since I was a kid. It's a good stress reliever."

"Hmm," she grunted. "Never took you for a ripped, heaving bodice type."

"I've ripped plenty of my own," he winked. "No, I like thriller."

"Really? Me too," she perked up. "What do you have there?" she indicated the book.

"Jameson's latest."

Gasping, she scrambled across the bed and snatched it up, looking at the cover then clutched it to her chest and looked up at him.

"I have been waiting for this!" she said. "I didn't think it was out yet."

"It's not," he replied.

"What? Then how did you get a copy?"

The side of his mouth quirked up. "Magic."

"Seriously, Paddy, how?" she gazed at the cover again and gently ran a hand over it.

"It's a secret," he teased.

"He's my favorite author," she admitted. "How did I not know you liked him?"

Paddy shrugged. "Since you're the first woman besides my doctor who has seen me in my reading glasses, I'm not surprised. No one knows I like to read."

"Why not?"

"I'm a player, a bad boy. Don't you listen to gossip?" he teased. "We aren't supposed to read."

"That's shite," she answered. "Have you read *The President's Secret*?"

"Read it?" he chuckled then held up one finger and left the room. Coming back with the book in his hand, he showed her. "I've read it, about five times." Handing it to her, she opened the cover and immediately, he regretted it.

"Oh my god, you have a signed copy?" she gushed. He cleared his throat and took his teacup taking a drink.

"I'd forgotten that."

"*To my boy, Paddy. Thanks for all the help. T.S. Jameson.* Do you know him?" she looked up.

"No, no," he answered too quickly. "He meant *support* but wrote *help*. He joked about it."

She eyed him. "It says *to my boy*. What aren't you telling me, O'Shea?" She handed it back and took the other one again.

"Nothing," he said. "Hey, why don't you eat. You're welcome to a shower, if you want. I have some sweatpants you can wear."

She nodded slowly. "Food and shower sounds amazing."

"Well, then," he offered to take the new release book back. When she held the book to her chest, he laughed. "Let me finish it and you can borrow it."

"Really?" she questioned.

"Sure, but I have to finish it first."

Her lips twisted in disappointment. "How long will it take you?"

"My my, is that a little green monster I see in your eyes?"

In true adult fashion, she stuck her tongue out at him. Chuckling, he crawled up the bed. She lay back allowing him to hover over her. The look in her eyes darkened and he knew he had won. Slowly lowering his lips to hers, he grinned when her eyes closed.

Snatching the book away from her and shimming down the bed away from her, he laughed at the indignation on her face. "Eat."

Huffing, she dramatically grabbed the sandwich and took a bite.

"Good girl," he teased.

She grabbed one of the pillows and chucked it at him. Laughing, he blocked the fluffy white pillow and bowed out of the room.

"Paddy," she called him back. Looking through the doorway, he waited. "Thank you."

He smiled at her and nodded once, slowly closing the door behind him.

Now, he sat beside her at the doctor's office waiting for the results. If she was pregnant, he wasn't sure what would happen between them. But he was certain of one thing, he couldn't let her go back to Patrick O'Flannery.

There was a knock on the door and Keera squeaked. Paddy sat back and took her hand in his, giving it a reassuring squeeze. She looked over at him, her green eyes rimmed with fear and yet it was the soft look of love he latched on to.

The door opened and the old doctor shuffled his way in, his gait typical of an old country doctor.

"Well, good morning," he said looking around. "Or is it afternoon?" he pulled out the little round stool doctors always sat on. "I never can remember what time it is, always have my clock set to chime when it's time for tea, like. It's not time yet, though," he sat and once situated, he sighed and looked over his thick, plastic-rimmed glasses to the three of them. "It's not every day I get so many visitors in one room. Now, what can I do for you?"

Keera looked at her mother, then Paddy, the look of confusion and the doctor's attitude irritated him.

"Your office called my daughter, Dr. Pierce," her mother started.

"We did? Dear me, are you all right?" he asked.

"Oh, for god's sake," Paddy muttered.

"Paddy, please," Keera begged.

"I'm sorry but he's incompetent," he stated.

The doctor didn't seem to hear him. Siobhan ignored their side conversation and looked at the doctor.

"We came here a couple days ago, Doctor. We were told my daughter's results were ready."

"Results?" he asked.

"The pregnancy results."

"Who's pregnant?" he looked between Siobhan and Keera and his eyes even looked at Paddy.

"Oh, for Christ's sake," Paddy stood. "Is there someone else we can speak to?"

Dr. Pierce looked up at him, surprised. "Now, now young man, there's no need to be nasty."

"Nasty? You haven't seen nasty, Doctor. You do not deserve that title and it's about time you retire if you can't even remember what your patients' needs are."

"Paddy, please, this isn't helping," Siobhan said.

"I know you want to know as much as I do, but Paddy, please," Keera said.

With a huff, he sat back down and grit his teeth.

"Dr. Pierce, we just need to know. Am I pregnant or not?" she asked. "I am late and took a pregnancy test at home. But I need to know for a fact. Please, can you let me know what the results are?"

Dr. Pierce looked at her for a moment then gave an absentminded grandfatherly smile and opened her file.

Chapter

Five

Keera appreciated why Paddy was so frustrated. She was too but being frustrated at the doctor was not going to move things along any faster.

As soon as the doctor opened her file, her hands went clammy and her mouth instantly went dry.

"Well," he started. "According to this, it looks like you are... goodness, you're so young."

Keera resisted groaning in frustration. Paddy huffed beside her. "Thank you, but that's not why we're here."

"Right right, of course," he waved her off and took his time pursuing the file. Finally, he looked up. "Unfortunately, my dear, it looks like you and your husband will have to keep trying for a baby. We do have some fertility specialists who could help if you would like me to recommend... goodness, my dear, you've gone quiet pale. It's nothing to worry about. I'm sure I'll have better news for you both at a later date."

Keera's ears were ringing, and her face had gone numb. Was she hearing him correctly?

"Are you..." she cleared her throat. "Are you saying I am *not* pregnant?"

He shook his head. "I'm sorry, my dear."

She forced her mind to clear. "No, no, that's fine but I took an at home pregnancy test and it was positive."

"At home tests can give a false positive for many reasons and the late cycle could mean you're stressed or perhaps had a reaction to birth control. Are you on it?"

She shook her head. "Not anymore. I stopped about a month ago." Right after she and Patrick O'Flannery broke up.

"It can cause symptoms like that and give false positives. I'm sorry I don't have better news for you both."

Keera couldn't reply. She had psyched herself up for a positive, she wasn't sure what to do with a negative. Paddy took her hand as her mom thanked the doctor.

She went through the motions of checking out and walking to the entrance. The fresh air filled her lungs and she felt tears on her cheeks. Paddy took her hand in his and turned her to face him. His eyes were shadowed, and she couldn't discern his emotions. He was so wonderful and had promised to take care of her and the baby but now there was no baby. Was there even a *them*?

He took her head in his hands and stared into her eyes, then just like that, he dropped his hold and looked over her shoulder.

Keera nearly screamed for him to hold her again, but he waited and soon her mother's comforting hand slipped into hers.

"Well, my dear," she said. "Are you all right?"

Keera nodded but one look at Paddy and she wasn't. It was selfish, but without a baby, she may have her life back, but she didn't have the love of her life back.

That thought stopped her dead in her tracks. She couldn't love Paddy. No, she couldn't. They may have been together a couple years, but it was never a serious thing. Besides, Paddy had never wanted a girlfriend. He liked his freedom. At least that was what he told her the morning after their first time together when he called her *cute but young.*

Shaking out of her memories that would only complicate things, she looked over at him again. His light brown, auburn hair caught the rays of sunlight between the clouds. His brown eyes still unreadable. He was that ray of sunlight in her cloudy life and now she had a glimpse the night before what it would be like with him but, was he only there because he thought she needed his help with the baby or was he there for her?

"I should get going," he said.

Not for her then.

"Thank you for coming today, Paddy," her mother said. He forced a smile.

"Of course," he answered.

"You should come over to dinner," Siobhan invited.

His eyes flashed to Keera, as she watched her world fall apart.

"I'd like that if you want me," he sounded so unsure. But he wanted to. Keera's body warmed to his words and boldly, she marched over to him, grabbed his face between her hands and kissed him soundly.

She didn't pull back until she heard her mother's phone ring. She looked up at Paddy to see his soft smile, but soon her mother's words on the phone distracted her.

"Oh, thank god," she sighed. Keera turned to look at her

mother. Paddy wrapped his arms round her, and she leaned back into him. They both said nothing as her mother continued. "What?" she demanded. "What do you mean she left him? Where is she? No, I'm going to talk to her. She will not put Emmet through this and get away with it… fine. No, we'll come over now."

Siobhan hung up the phone and looked over at them. "Emmet's awake," she announced.

"Oh, thank god," both Paddy and Keera said together.

"There's more," Siobhan continued. "It looks like Mara left him."

"Left him? Like, left him in the hospital while she goes home?" Keera asked.

"No, like, left him, annulled the marriage."

"She can't do that!" Keera looked over at Paddy. "Can she?"

"It's not illegal," Paddy replied. "But Emmet's going to be devastated. He just got his family."

"Dee was in tears when she told me. I should go back to the hospital. Paddy, could you take Keera home?"

"Of course," he agreed. "Unless," he turned to Keera and she was grateful. "Do you want to go see him?"

Keera nodded. But Siobhan was already pulling out her keys.

"We're right behind you, ma," Keera said. Siobhan nodded and with a distracted smile, headed to her car, got in, and drove away.

Keera looked up at Paddy who was watching her intently. "I know with everything going on, we haven't really talked. I want to go see my friend, but… are you okay?"

"With not being pregnant?" He nodded and she continued. "I'll not deny it's a relief but there was a time I was… prepared. I didn't want to be because I have dreams and want to explore them before settling down with a kid, but I had come to terms with it. I didn't think I ever wanted to be a mother, not that my ma isn't an amazing mother, I just didn't think I'd be a good mother. But now, I see you and I think… there's only one I would want to be the father of any future kids I may have and that's you, Paddy."

He stared down at her, his expression unreadable but a myriad of emotions flickered across his eyes.

"I feel the same," he finally said and took her in his arms, kissing the top of her head. "But you're wrong, you know. You'll be an amazing ma, so you will."

She relaxed into him and gripped his back tightly.

"I love you, Keera O'Quinn."

She buried her nose into his shirt and took a deep sniff of his cologne.

"Enough to let me borrow TS Jameson's latest book now?" she teased and reveled in the rumble in his chest.

"I love you, but not that much."

She pulled back with an "och" and smacked his arm. He winked but gently pulled her chin up to him.

"I do love you, Keera."

"I love you too, Paddy O'Shea," she admitted suddenly serious. "But now, we need to face my cousins and help Emmet in any way we can."

"Emmet yes, telling your cousins?" he grimaced and covered his lower region with his hand. "Not sure. I'm rather fond of this part of me."

She grinned, went up on her toes and kissed him quickly. "Me too," she teased. "Don't worry, I'll protect it."

Paddy chuckled and brushed her chin with the backs of his fingers.

"Have I told you how crazy you are?"

"Not today," she shrugged. "I'm actually surprised."

"Well, you are love. Now, let's get going. The faster we get to the hospital, the sooner the beating I'm going to get from your cousins will be over."

They walked to his car and after he held the door for her, he slid in beside her and started the car.

"Let's not tell Emmet," she said. "I want to tell everyone but after what she did, he's probably not interested in anyone's happiness."

"Agreed," he put the car in gear and slowly eased out of the parking lot, heading to the hospital.

Chapter

Six

Hurrying through the door and down the hall to Emmet's room, Paddy and Keera looked for her family. Spying her mom and Emmet's parents, they headed that way. Everyone looked up when they arrived. Orin's eyes went immediately down to their clasped hands then back up at Keera and raised an eyebrow.

"Oh, sweetie," Deirdre said and rushed to take her into her arms. "How are you feeling, sweetie? Can we get you anything? A glass of water? Sit down, sit down. Oh, hello Paddy, dear. Come sit."

"Auntie, I'm fine." Keera stopped her aunt from walking her over to the bench. "I'm sorry, but I'm not pregnant."

"Not? But I thought..."

"I thought so too," she embarrassingly looked over at her Uncle Orin who promptly dropped a hand on Paddy's shoulder and asked to have him join him in the cafeteria. When the men left, Keera looked up at her aunt. "I was late, and I took a test. The test said positive, but ma and I went to the doctor and he just got the medical test back. Mine was a false positive. I'm not pregnant. I'm sorry."

"Oh sweetie, don't be sorry," Deirdre said. "You weren't ready. I could tell you were nervous. It's always better with the right man by your side."

Keera smiled. "You've probably already guessed, Auntie, but Paddy and I are together."

"I noticed," she said. "But since when? I thought Patrick O'Flannery was your beau."

"Sort of. Paddy and I started dating my final year of school before I went to university. We haven't been together for about two years. But I've always loved him."

"Well, dear, I'm glad," Deirdre said. "He's a nice young man. You'll be very happy with him. When's the wedding?"

Keera nearly choked on her own saliva. "Ehm..."

"Come now, Deirdre," Siobhan scolded. "Enough of that. Don't push."

"Push? I would never!"

"Aren't those Emmet's son's grandparents?" Keera asked changing the subject and indicating the older couple walking to them with a sleeping Trevor in their arms.

"Yes," Deirdre replied and waved them over.

"Any news?" the grandmother, Keera forgot her name, asked.

"He's resting," Deirdre said. "Cabhan is with him. They gave him a sedative while they fix the damage he did ripping his stitches."

"Oh goodness," the grandmother gasped.

"I swear if I ever see that woman again, she better run the other way for everything she put my Emmet through. 'Tis unseemly!" Deirdre cried.

"I agree," the grandmother replied in a huff, sitting beside Deirdre. "I know we didn't make his time easy, but she should have known. What sort of woman leaves her man alone when he needs her the most?"

"We don't know her side of things," Siobhan said. "Now, I love Emmet and I don't believe anyone deserves that but… we do need to know her side. We hated you and Curtis for a little while, but once we knew your side of things, Joann. We've grown to care for you both."

"Thank you," Joann, the grandmother said. "But I'll be the first to say you had every right to hate us," she glanced up at her husband crossly.

"It was her ex who shot him. Maybe she's scared or trying to protect him," Keera offered.

"Still," Deirdre replied. "She better not show her face when I'm around."

"Grampa," little Trevor said groggily as he slowly woke from his grandfather's shoulder. "When can I see Daddy?"

"Soon, son," he answered. "Your daddy needs to rest."

Trevor nodded his little head, huffed a sigh, and yawned. Resting his head against his grandfather's shoulder again, he was asleep in minutes.

"I'm going to take him back to the hotel," he said. "Call me if something changes."

His wife nodded and watched them go.

"When's your flight, Joann?" Deirdre asked.

"We were supposed to fly out after the hearing, but we extended the time. We aren't leaving for another week or so," she explained. "But now that Emmet's in the hospital and he has custody of Trevor, I don't know… I don't want him to worry about doing too much too fast and Trevor can be a handful."

Before anyone got a chance to reply, Paddy and Orin came back, carrying cups of tea and coffee for everyone. Keera searched Paddy's gaze to see what her uncle had said to him, but when he smiled at her, she relaxed. It couldn't have been too bad.

Orin took the last two cups, "I'm going to give this to Cabhan and check on Em."

The women nodded and Paddy sat beside Keera.

"What happened?" She whispered as the three older women started talking together. Paddy took a sip of his tea and shrugged.

"Nothing much," he replied. "He merely asked me my intentions toward you and made it clear you were like a daughter to him, so I better watch out."

"Ugh," she groaned and lowered her head to her hands. "I'm sorry, why does my family have to treat me like a child?"

"Wanting to protect you isn't treating you like a child," he answered. "They care about you. Love you. And when I told him how I felt about you, he made mention of my... less than pleasant reputation with women and I told him I was young and stupid. I'm not as young and not as stupid as I was and gave my word, I would be faithful to you. He dropped it and we got the drinks."

Keera locked eyes with him and smiled slightly. "Two down, and it feels like a thousand to go."

"We don't have to do it all now, you know," he offered. "We can wait. I'm not going anywhere, love."

The endearment sent a shiver down her spine. She'd missed him. Leaning over, she kissed him quickly just as the door opened and her eldest cousin, Cabhan walked out. Freezing in the doorway, he stared at them. Keera blushed a deep red and pulled away from Paddy.

"Is he awake?" Deirdre jumped up and went to her stepson.

"Ehm, aye," Cabhan replied, his eyes still on Keera and Paddy.

"Thank god," Deirdre pushed passed him and rushed into the hospital room. Trevor's grandmother pulled out her phone and called her husband.

"How long?" Cabhan asked them, ignoring everything else.

"We've been dating since I turned eighteen, stopped for two years when I went to college and just picked back up again," Keera explained.

"And you were going to tell us... when?" Cabhan demanded.

"When I was good and ready," she replied. "I don't need a da', Cabhan."

"Maybe you do."

"Nope, sure don't. Thanks, though." She stood, pushed past him and tried to enter the hospital room.

"How do you think Emmet will feel about this?" he questioned.

"Feel about what?" Emmet's voice demanded. The harsh tone was unlike any she'd ever heard from her favorite cousin. In truth, all her cousins were her favorite, but Emmet held a special place.

Frozen in the doorway, she met his intense gaze. She said and did nothing but when she felt Paddy walk up behind her, she leaned back into him, for comfort. Emmet's eyes twitched.

"What in the bloody hell is going on?" He roared.

"Em, please," Paddy started. "Let me explain."

"Are you shagging my cousin?" he bellowed.

"Emmet," Deirdre reproached.

He ignored her. "Answer me!"

Paddy took a deep breath, but Keera continued. "So what if he is? What does it matter?"

"Are you?" Emmet did not drop Paddy's gaze.

"We have slept together in the past, but I fail to understand—"

"Get out of my sight. And don't bother going back to the dealership. You're fired," Emmet stated.

"Emmet," Keera gasped. "You can't do that. Not to Paddy. He's your friend."

"He *was* my friend. Friends don't go behind your back. Friends don't sneak around. Friends don't betray you!"

"I never meant to betray you, Emmet. Keera and I—"

"I said get out!" Emmet shouted.

Paddy took a step back and Keera turned to look up at him.

"Please, don't," she begged.

"I'll not be gone for good. I think we need to let him cool off," Paddy said. "I'll see you soon. Okay?"

Keera nodded and watched him leave. Not realizing why tears were streaming down her cheeks until he glanced back at her. She wiped furiously at her face and turned to Emmet.

"I've always been there for you! I have always helped you without any hesitation and you couldn't do one little thing for me?" She demanded. "Maybe that's why the bullet missed your heart. Maybe you don't have one!"

"Keera," her mother snapped but Keera ran out of the hospital room and out the door to see Paddy's car driving off.

Paddy didn't know where he was going, all he knew was he had to go somewhere, anywhere. It's not as if he didn't know Emmet's reactions would be intense, but he did not expect it to be borderline psychotic. He expected a fight, not to be fired. Not that it mattered. He'd find another job. He had skills and he was all right financially. If needed, he could visit his uncle in Limerick. Uncle Tully raised him after his parents died. But what bothered him the most was the toll it would take on Keera. She may hide it well, but Emmet had hurt her. It had hurt him too when Emmet denied him, but he knew Em would come around. He had too. Paddy wasn't going anywhere.

When the dealership came into view, Paddy sighed and turned in. He hoped Emmet wasn't serious about firing him. The dealership was his home away from home. He was close to the guys and enjoyed working there. Parking in his usual spot, he got out and headed inside. Tom met him at the door. For a second, Paddy worried Emmet had called and banned him from the property but then Tom asked how Emmet was doing.

"I saw you pull in. How is he?"

"Is it just you?" Paddy asked looking around the quiet space.

"It is, yeah," Tom answered.

"Good," Paddy replied. "Care for a pint?"

Tom's brows rose but he glanced at the clock. Ten minutes to six, they could lock up.

"Sure," Tom agreed. "Everything all right?"

"I... ehm... can't believe I'm about to ask this, but I need some advice."

"All right," Tom nodded. "Let me get my coat."

Paddy watched him go into his office and grab his suit coat then flick off the lights.

"Got everything?" he asked. "Aren't you opening tomorrow?"

"I honestly don't know," Paddy said. "Come on. I'll tell you everything once I have a beer in my hand."

Tom said nothing, only followed him out and locked up.

Chapter

Seven

Finding a spot at the bar in a pub, walking distance from their work, Tom and Paddy slid onto the barstools and ordered two pints. Staying silent until they were served, they cheersed and Paddy took a long draw on the Guinness.

"Wanna tell me what's going on?" Tom asked.

"Emmet's awake," he led with the good news.

"Grand," Tom smiled. "But that's not why you have that tight expression on your face. What happened?"

"Do you know where Mara is?" he asked.

Tom's eyes quivered for a moment, then he took another sip. "Possibly, why?"

"She told you then?" Paddy asked.

"Chloe," Tom corrected.

"I'm not judging anyone, but she needs to talk to Emmet. He's gutted."

"She's a grown woman. She has her reasons."

"Then tell Emmet those reasons. If she can't, then can I talk to her?"

Tom huffed a sigh. "Come back with me and we'll see, but if she doesn't want to, we can't force her."

"Understood."

"Now, want to get to the part where you tell me what's going on with you?" Tom asked. "We were friends once."

"We were and I owe your wife and apology for my rude behavior when I met her at the dealership a few weeks ago."

"Yeah, she mentioned that."

Paddy sighed. "I didn't know the whole story. I blindly believed it was Chloe's fault she and Emmet broke up all those years ago, but my rudeness was because I had just gotten out of a relationship that ended badly."

"I understand. I do. And she does too. But what's up now? Girl trouble again?"

"Emmet's cousin, Keera and I are in a relationship," he finally admitted. Tom leaned back and stared at him.

"No shit, really?"

Paddy nodded. "Started when she was eighteen. We took a break for two years when she went to America for Uni and I met someone else. That ended quickly but when Keera got back, we picked back up. We had a fight about fifteen months back and decided to call it quits. We just got back together, and I love her."

"But Emmet is livid," Tom guessed. "I'm happy for you. But I remember how protective he was toward his cousin. You play with fire."

"Yeah, I got that when he found out and fired me."

"What?" Tom questioned. "Seriously?" Paddy nodded and sighed. "Shite. Will you be okay?"

"I'm hoping after a cool down, he'll see reason."

Tom sucked his teeth and shrugged. "Honestly, I doubt it. He's so protective of her. I don't know."

"Yeah I know. But I'm not going anywhere. I love Keera and I love Emmet as a brother. He's hurting."

"Yeah, I know," Tom answered. "Look let's settle up here and follow me home. We'll talk to Mara together, *if* she'll talk."

Paddy agreed and downed his beer.

"You'll be fine," Tom slapped him on the back. "Let's go and get this settled. I'm sure with a little push, Mara will see reason. She loves him."

"Well, let's just hope it doesn't take her years to realize her mistake."

"Here's to hoping."

Keera wrapped her arms tighter around herself. The sun hid behind the clouds and though it was warm earlier in the day, the gathering clouds lowered the temperature to well below sixty degrees… Shaking her head, she corrected; fifteen degrees. She couldn't seem to shake the Americanisms even though she had been back over a year.

Walking back to her Aunt's and Uncle's hadn't been her best idea but it was all she could do. She couldn't stay there with Emmet. He hurt her deeply. She still couldn't believe he had fired Paddy. Thinking of him, she realized she could have called him but didn't know how he felt about her after Emmet. She had gotten him fired. Tears rolled down her cheeks.

A car slowed behind her and she tried to calm her heartbeat.

"Honey," it was her mom. She breathed a sigh of relief. "Were you going to walk all the way to your Uncle's?"

Keera looked over and sniffled. "Yeah."

"Oh honey, you don't even have a key. Come on, get in. Let's talk."

"You're going to defend Emmet and I can't hear that right now."

"You don't know that. Come on. Get in."

Keera debated when she felt large drops fall on her arm. Finally, she agreed and got in. They were quiet for a long moment until Siobhan broke the silence.

"He was absolutely wrong for what he did to Paddy. But, and this is in no way defending him, he doesn't know your relationship with him. He doesn't know what he's done for you. And not only that, love, he just lost everything."

"Wrong," Keera spat. "He lost some scheming skank. He still has us. He still has his son and dammit, he's still alive!"

"I know, sweetie, but think about it this way... Imagine Paddy coming over and saying he never loved you and he leaves without explanation. Say he says you were a mistake and he couldn't be a father to your child. Think how you would feel..."

Keera heaved a sigh. It wasn't too long ago she was afraid of that very scenario happening.

"But that doesn't give him the right—"

"No, you're right. But one thing, honey, you have to understand, and I know it's not something you want to hear but he loves you so much and maybe he knows more about Paddy than you do. Maybe there's history there. Who knows, but when he's able to get past his own woes, he will be able to see that. You just have to give him some time. Don't hate him. He can't lose you too."

Keera burst into tears. Her heart hurt for him. Everything he went through and then she yelled at him and made it worse.

"Oh, ma," she sobbed. Siobhan pulled off the road, parked and pulled Keera into her arms.

"Shh, shh, it's all right, love," she soothed.

"I'm so sorry for what I said to him," she cried. "Everything... it's just... so much."

"I know, honey, I know. Cry it out, it's all right, but don't make yourself sick."

Keera cried for a little while letting her mom hold her. Finally, when her tears subsided, she pulled away from her and looked into her eyes.

"Where do you want to go, love?" Siobhan asked.

"Can we go back to the hospital? I need to apologize to Em."

"Of course we can," Siobhan kissed her forehead, settled back in her seat and put the car in gear.

"Then I want to find that woman and beat the ever-loving shite out of her," Keera muttered.

"I intend to join you," Siobhan agreed and pulled out into the traffic.

Chapter Eight

Paddy followed Tom as he pulled off the main road and onto his street. Remembering the way since it was the same house Tom grew up in, Paddy pulled in behind Tom's car. They both got out and headed toward the front door which opened, and Tom's three children raced out to greet him.

"Daddy!" they all cried excitedly and jumped on him. Tom laughed and held on to as many as he could.

"I missed you, Daddy," his daughter stated.

"I missed you too, sweetheart," he picked her up and kissed her cheek.

Paddy felt a pang of need race through him, seeing Tom with his children. He never thought about being a father since his own died when he was so young, but when he heard Keera could have been pregnant, his world turned completely.

Seeing Tom interact with the three and following Tom's gaze when he looked up at the front door to see Chloe, seven months pregnant but glowing with love as she gazed at her husband, Paddy knew what he wanted. Keera.

A smile lifted his lips when he thought about her. She told him she loved him, and he loved her. Why couldn't they have the same as Tom and Chloe?

Chloe's eyes turned to him and her brows furrowed in confusion. Clearing his throat softly, he followed Tom and the kids up the steep incline and to the door. The kids rushed on in, but Tom, Chloe, and Paddy stood together.

"What's happened?" she questioned.

"Emmet's awake again," Tom encouraged. "But there's been some... talk."

She glanced at him and he felt like an arse all over again. The last time she saw him, he had accused her of things he knew nothing about.

"Talk?" she questioned.

"Is Mara home?" Tom asked.

Chloe bit her lip clearly debating on telling them.

"Please, Chloe," Paddy pleaded. "I am not here to judge anyone. I know I haven't shown that before and I'm so sorry. I didn't know everything that happened between you and Emmet and I am sorry for what I said to you last month. That's partly why I am here now. I never want to make the same mistake. I want to speak with Mara and get to the bottom of this. My best friend is hurting. He loves her so much and I don't want him to hurt anymore. Not if I can do something about it."

Chloe stared at him then huffed. "Okay, come in. Let's see if she'll talk."

"Thank you," Paddy said. As soon as they entered, Paddy looked up to see Mara standing on the steps. Her face was pale, and her arms were wrapped around herself, almost as if she was cold but Paddy knew better than that. "Mara," he started.

"What are you doing here?" she questioned.

"I came to talk to you," he said. "Emmet's in a bad way. Can you tell me what's going on? I just want to hear your side."

Worry entered her eyes for a moment, then was replaced by a cool mask of indifference. She shrugged; it was forced but it was cold.

"I don't love him. It was a mistake to get married so quickly. I didn't realize it until he nearly died, then I would have had to raise his son. I'm not ready to be a mother. It's over."

Paddy bit back his initial response which would have been that her reply was canned and a lie. He couldn't say that. He had to be indifferent and remain calm.

"Can I ask if this sudden change has anything to do with your ex shooting him?" She flinched and he knew he'd hit home. "You know he doesn't blame you for that, right?"

Again, she shrugged. "It doesn't matter."

"Mara," he took a tentative step toward her. She went up one stair.

"I'm sorry he's in the hospital and I'm sorry he's hurt, but it's better this happened now than ten years from now," she turned to go.

"He ripped his stitches," Paddy tried one last time. This time with guilt. She froze, not turning. "When you left, he tried to follow you. Both stitches ripped. I heard he bled down the entire front of his hospital gown before his brother Cabhan caught him and got him to the bed." Her back shook and he knew enough about women to know she was holding back tears. "Even through all of that, his one shout was begging his brother to tell him it wasn't true, that you *did* love him, that you were just scared. He held to that, even when they upped his morphine to knock him out so they could assess his wounds and restitch them. He loves you, Mara. I can only imagine how much he loves you. And here you are, claiming what you felt was fake? I beg you, reconsider. For his sake as well as yours. He is a good man who loves you. If you're scared, you can both work it out. Please, Mara."

Paddy went quiet, allowing her to think. Mara stood frozen, her back to him for several moments. Then, she took a deep breath. She said nothing, only climbed the stairs slowly, disappearing around the curve of the steps and into her room. He heard the door shut and cursed.

"I'm proud of you," Keera's mom whispered as they stood at Emmet's hospital room door.

"Let me go in alone?" she asked.

"Of course," Siobhan nodded. Keera thanked her and knocked on the door, waiting.

Cabhan opened the door, his eyes widening slightly when he saw her.

"Is he awake?" Keera asked. Cabhan nodded, smiling softly.

"And been asking for you. He feels badly for how he spoke to you." Keera made a move to enter the room when her cousin stepped in front. "Go easy, Kee, he's not himself and needs to keep his blood pressure down."

Keera nodded. Then, with a glance at her mom, she stepped around Cabhan and into Emmet's hospital room.

The smell of disinfectant hit her hard, but she tried not to gag. Emmet's eyes were closed but his breathing was irregular, showing he was awake just resting. All the hospital machine hookups made her eyes water. Emmet was larger than life. The biggest of her cousins in physique but also in personality. She loved him. He was never supposed to be hurt. He was invincible. She sniffled and he opened his eyes. Looking toward her, he sighed in relief and a tired, hurt smile ghosted across his lips.

"Kee," he breathed then cleared his throat. Attempting to sit up, he let Cabhan raise the bed, instead of fighting the pain. "Honey, I'm so sorry for what I said and how I behaved."

"No, *I'm* sorry, Em. I said horrible things to you."

"I deserved them."

"No, you didn't," she shook her head. "I can only imagine what you're going through."

"It doesn't excuse me treating you that way. It surprised me, is all. I didn't know you even knew who Paddy was."

"We met at your thirtieth birthday party, but we didn't start dating until I was eighteen."

"Clearly, it's ehm... serious?"

She nodded. "I love him, and he loves me."

Emmet grimaced and Keera bit her lip. "Love," he scoffed. "Just make sure he actually means it."

"Mara meant it too," Keera said. Emmet flinched. "In her own way."

"Yeah, well..." he took her hand in his and kissed it. "So long as he respects you and doesn't hurt you, I'm okay with it."

"You have no idea," she smiled. Looking down, knowing he would never judge her, she continued. "I thought I was pregnant."

Emmet started and Cabhan coughed up the water he was drinking.

"By Paddy?"

She shook her head and glanced at Cabhan then back at Emmet. "Patrick O'Flannery. My sometimes boyfriend. I took a test at home that day you announced... you and..." Emmet nodded understanding. She couldn't say it was the day he announced he was going to marry Mara. It would hurt him too much.

"I wondered why you were so upset that day."

"It was a positive result and I truly thought I was... Paddy was here when my mom let it slip and... when we talked, he offered to help me raise the child as his own since Patrick would make a horrible father and we're over anyway." Tears pooled in her eyes. Emmet blinked, trying to process. "He came with me when ma and I went to the doctor and it seems the test I took at home gave me a false positive. I'm not pregnant but Paddy was there. He would have raised my child. He..." she stopped and looked down as her throat closed. "He said he loved me, no matter what."

"Dear god," Emmet breathed, his eyes trailing over her shoulder to the white wall behind her. He shook himself out of his thoughts and cupped her jaw. "I'm sorry you went through that, love."

"It's my own fault. But Paddy..."

"Didn't deserve anything I said to him," Emmet admitted. "I... I'm sorry. This – ehm – whole thing has—"

"You don't need to say anything. We both understand."

Emmet nodded as tears gathered in the corners of his eyes. "I love you, Kee. And I'll always be there for you but I'm glad you have someone who will pick up where I can't." He tried to wink but the sight only caused her chest to constrict even more.

"I love you too, Em," she replied. "And I'm so sorry you're hurt. I'm here to help, in any way I can."

He said nothing only reached for her hand. She leaned over him and embraced him as best she could with the IV, EKG, and oxygen monitor hookups on his body. She cried into his shoulder, thanking providence he was still with her. She felt his tears through the shoulder of her shirt. Saying nothing, she let him cry and, before pulling back, wiped her tears.

Looking at him, the glistening in his eyes and the tracks

on his cheeks made her sob. He wiped the tears from her face and smiled as best he could.

"Now, go find him. Tell him I need to talk to him," Emmet said.

She nodded and leaned her head down so he could kiss her forehead.

"You'll be okay?" she asked.

He forced a smile. "Always am. Besides we're O'Quinns, we make the best of it."

A knock at the door stopped her from responding. The door opened and Trevor's grandfather walked in, carrying Trevor in his arms.

"Oh, sorry, bad time?" he asked.

"Daddy!" Trevor cried.

The first genuine smile in a while crossed Emmet's lips as he looked at his son.

"I was just leaving," Keera said.

"We can come back," the grandfather said.

"No! I wanna see my daddy," Trevor protested.

"It's fine," she smiled at him then turned back to Emmet. "Just remember what you have remaining."

Emmet nodded and squeezed her hand. As she left, she glanced back to see Trevor climb up on Emmet's bed with Cabhan's help and hug his father. Emmet still had an emptiness in his eyes, but they brightened slightly as he held his son. Cabhan caught her eyes and smiled. Her favorite thing about being one of two girls in the family, was that all the older male cousins were protective but most importantly, nonjudgmental. Cabhan just heard everything she told Emmet and she knew he would never judge her either. Keera and her cousin, their sister, Sinéad often talked about it. The O'Quinn lads always looked after them, now it was her turn. She needed to see happiness in Emmet's eyes again. She needed a partner in crime, and Sinéad was a text away.

Keera: Sinéad, we need to talk. Battle strategy.

Sinéad: I'm in, Kee, who are we killing today?

Keera laughed. Sinéad was one of her best friends and always teased.

Keera: Codename: the bitch.

Sinéad: Ooh, yass! I'm in. What's the plan?

Keera: I'm going to meet with Paddy to see if he knows anything. He's friends with Tom. AKA the bitch's brother-in-law.

Sinéad: I'd offer to meet with you, but I don't want to see the whole PDA thing between you two.

Keera: Whatever, count yourself fortunate you knew before your brothers.

Sinéad: THEY KNOW? How? How did they take it?

Keera: Cabh and Em know that's it. At first, it was how you'd expect, then we talked. They understand.

Sinéad: Wow, babe, sorry! Glad you finally told them. It was getting difficult to not tell them now I'm back from Oz.

Keera: Thanks for keeping it a secret.

Sinéad: Of course! Hey! Maybe now it's out there, we can double date! Brody would love to meet him.

Keera: Yeah, that'd be good. But until we figure out Emmet's situation, let's hold off, aye?

Sinéad: Okay, your sergeant at arms is ready for your command, chief. Let me know what's needed and it'll get done.

Keera: No questions will be asked. I have to have plausible deniability, haha.

Sinéad: Ha! Yes, Madame President. Understood. SAA out.

Keera: SAA?

Sinéad: Sergeant at arms? Duh. And I'm not the one who lived in America.

Keera: Ooh, got it. I'll text you later.

Switching over to Paddy's text chain, she typed out a message.

Keera: Where are you?

Paddy: Just leaving Tom's and Chloe's. Why?"

Keera: Good! Is Mara there?

Paddy: Yes, but she isn't talking. She's scared by something, Kee.

Keera: She better be scared of me. But I talked to Emmet. He wants to talk to you soon but not now. He needs his rest.

Paddy: Should I bring a codpiece? You know, protect the important bits?

Keera: Haha, he's come around. But I need to bring Mara to him. He needs happiness again.

Paddy: Probably not going to happen. I'm afraid. She wouldn't talk to me and she hasn't talked to Chloe or Tom either. Looks like we will have to wait until she comes around.

Keera: I'm done waiting. I've already talked to Sinéad.

Paddy: Kee, think about this. We can't push her.

Keera: Like hell.

Paddy: Come on, love. You know I'm right. Let's talk. Should someone go over to Em's place and feed his dog?

Keera: He's staying with Uncle Orin and Aunt Dee. I'm going to check in on Ness and I'll meet you for lunch?

Paddy: Murphy's?

Keera: Give me an hour or so.

Paddy: See you there.

Keera: I love you.

Paddy: I love you!

Keera grinned. She may not be certain about getting Mara back to Emmet. She may not even be sure about the future with Paddy, but one thing she was absolutely sure of is, she would never grow tired of hearing Paddy O'Shea say those words to her.

Chapter

Nine

Paddy sat at one of the more intimate tables at Murphy's. The world-renowned pub was one locals enjoyed as well as tourists. The quint setting with stone walls, wooden beams, and historic trinkets made it the quintessential Irish pub. After a long day at work, either at the dealership or at the Plaza hotel, Paddy always walked over to College Street for a pint and some live music.

That afternoon, however, there were only a handful of people having lunch. His friend and bartender walked past him with a rag and a couple empty glasses.

"Slow afternoon, Seamus?" he asked.

"Aye, thank god," he sighed. "Me and Tan were run off our feet last night, so we were. Bus of tourists dropped off to the hotel last night. All wanted a taste of Ireland."

"Where are they now? Sleeping in?" Paddy teased.

"Hardly, up at eight for the jaunty car ride to Ross Castle."

"Ah, nice day for it."

"'Tis," Seamus agreed. Then his eyes glanced down at his half full glass. "Another?"

"Aye, cheers."

"Meeting someone?" Seamus asked, looking at the empty chair with a menu at the place.

"Aye, Keera."

Seamus' eyebrows rose. "Aye? Good on ya! Does she still drink her usual?"

"She does."

"I'll get her a pint," Seamus offered.

"Cheers."

The door opened and Paddy looked over. Keera entered, scanned the room and smiled when her eyes landed on him. His breath caught at the twinkle he saw there, and his hands felt clammy.

"What?" she questioned with a laugh. Only then did he realize he was standing and staring at her.

"Nothing," he shook himself out of his stupor. She sat in the empty seat, still looking up at him.

"Are you going to sit? Or are we going somewhere else?" she asked.

"Sorry," he sat and cleared his throat.

"Are you okay?" she asked.

"Yeah, sorry, it's just... I guess I'm a little nervous."

"Why?" she questioned.

"Well, we haven't been on a date in two years."

"Is this a date?" she questioned.

"Do you want it to be?"

"I don't know. I figured our date would be more than a pint and a sandwich."

"Oh, of course," he corrected. "Right now, we can just be two friends having lunch."

Keera smiled at him and turned her eyes to Seamus, who brought her pint. "Thank you, Seamus. It's good to see you."

"It's good to see you both together again. You know, since you two broke up, my lad here hasn't dated anyone," Seamus revealed.

Paddy felt his stomach flip when Keera's gaze snapped to him.

"I tell ya, I think he's besotted, like," Seamus grinned. "Now, what can I get ya?" he went on as if he hadn't just dropped the largest bomb on her. Paddy didn't hear what she ordered but when Seamus asked for his order, he simply said, *the same.* Once they were alone again, he looked at Keera.

"Is it true?" she asked.

"What?" he knew exactly what but pretended and took a sip of his water.

"Don't give me that," she said. "Is it true?"

"Ehm... I went on a couple dates and there was one somewhat serious early on, but yeah, nothing else."

Keera looked down and he would have given anything at that moment to know what shew as thinking.

They were silent for a few minutes until Keera spoke again.

"Emmet's going home today," she said.

"Good," Paddy replied. "I'm glad he's doing better."

"He wants to talk to you. He asked me to tell you to come over tonight. He's staying at his parent's house while he recovers. My aunt invited you to dinner. Will you come?"

"Yeah, of course," he replied.

"Maybe," she started, then looked down. "Maybe it would be a good time to tell my family about us?" she looked up at him. "Everyone will be there."

Paddy took a deep breath and covered her hand with his. After staring into her eyes for a long moment, he nodded. She smiled broadly and squeezed his hand.

"I'm sorry about earlier with Emmet. And I'm sorry how I ended things fifteen months ago. I was angry but I should have understood. I wasted so much time. I love you."

"I love you too, Keera, and I was an arse," Paddy said. "I'm just glad we had a second chance."

"Me too," she replied stroking her thumb over his knuckles.

Seamus brought their food and they settled back into their playful flirtatious routine.

Chapter

Ten

Keera's eyes kept drifting to the clock in the other room waiting for six o'clock to come. Emmet was on his way home with his father and eldest brother Cabhan. Keera, her mom, and her Aunt Deirdre along with Sinéad, her boyfriend, Trisha, and Racheal, two of her cousin's wives, were at Orin's and Deirdre's house helping prepare dinner. Everyone was quiet as the worry for Emmet grew. He was still surly with some but what worried Keera the most, was he had not actually cried and mourned for the loss. Yes, he cried to Cabhan but that was an hysterical pain just after Mara left.

The name still caused Keera to wince in distaste. That woman... she talked to Paddy at length about his visit to Tom's house to talk to her. All Paddy kept saying over and over again was that Mara was scared but he didn't know why. They had caught the bastard who shot Emmet, why didn't she go back to him?

Shaking her head, she sighed.

"What's wrong, love?" her mother asked, and all the women turned to look at her.

"Nothing," she replied. "Just worried for Emmet. I still don't understand why."

"We may never," Rachael, Cabhan's wife said. "But I can't imagine what they're both going through."

"I don't know about her," Keera's aunt Deirdre started. "But I know my Emmet is going through hell thanks to that woman."

"God forgive me, but I almost wish they don't get back together. Emmet could do so much better than her," Emmet's sister, Sinéad said. Her boyfriend stroked her arm in comfort.

"Same here, love," Siobhan replied.

They all went quiet as the door opened. Looking over, Keera watched her best friend Ness and her husband Sean walk in. Sean carried a car seat in one hand and a paisley diaper bag slung over his shoulder. Ness looked amazing... tired, but she glowed.

The women squealed and rushed to them, giving hugs but more focused on the tiny baby boy swaddled in a perfect onesie and blanket, asleep in the car seat.

"He's so perfect," Deirdre breathed staring at her grandson, tears filling her eyes. She turned back to Ness and wrapped an arm around her shoulders. "How do you feel, love?"

"Tired," Ness sighed. "But so thankful the delivery was so easy."

"Twelve hours isn't bad at all for your first child," Ness's mother Brenda stated from the doorway carrying a food container and smiling at her daughter. "I pulled in just as you two were walking in."

Kissing her daughter's cheek, she passed the dish to Sinéad and went to greet her other daughter, Trisha.

"Sean has been a godsend," Ness said. "I couldn't have done it without him."

Sean smiled up at his wife as he crouched down to take his son out of the car seat. With such love and gentleness, Sean cradled him to his chest, looking down in awe.

"Would anyone like to hold him?" Sean asked.

There was a unison *yes* then giggles. Sean passed his son, Liam to his stepmom first. Deirdre had held him before but there was something almost reverent about her holding him then.

Keera watched as the baby boy was passed from one to the other. Ness looked over at her.

"Do you want to hold him?" she asked. Keera's eyes grew wide when Trish turned to offer the little one.

"Ehm... I don't know how," she admitted.

"It's easy," Ness replied taking her son from her half-sister and demonstrated. "See?"

"Just support his neck and one hand under his bum," Sean explained.

Ness gently passed little Liam to her and Keera's heart raced. He felt so breakable. Finally, she relaxed as much as she could and felt a smile grow across her face. He was so precious. His little face relaxed in sleep; Keera couldn't pull her eyes away. She had a sense of fulfillment come over her. A little boy with Paddy's golden eyes or his particular shade of brown hair. Her lips parted as an ache built in her core. She never wanted children before but with the thought of Paddy being their father, a deep-seated need echoed inside her.

Just then, there was a knock at the door. Deirdre went to open it and smiled.

"Paddy, dear, welcome!" she said, and Keera's ache

increased tenfold.

"Sorry for being early," his voice sent a shiver down her. "I wanted to see if I could help in anyway. Heavy lifting of helping Emmet."

"That is so sweet of you," Deirdre said. "Come in. They're not here yet. We're gushing over my new grandson. Have you met Liam yet?"

"No, not yet," he said. Keera's eyes were on the front door. He was still outside, and she wanted to see him so very much.

"Well, come in, come in," Deirdre stepped aside, and Paddy walked in. His eyes scanned the group and froze on her. His mouth dropped open, his whiskey colored eyes dilated, and he licked his lips. Keera rocked little Liam as their eyes locked. The urge to kiss him hit her hard. Without thought, she walked straight over to him, baby in her arms, rose to her tiptoes, and kissed him full on his luscious lips.

His taste hit home and she sighed. Spearmint, a hint of beer, and all Paddy. Pulling away, she blushed when Liam squirmed in her arms, now clearly awake. Everyone watched them and waited.

Paddy's sexy half grin lifted the corner of his mouth.

"I missed you," she whispered.

He could say nothing because Ness walked over to her. "I knew it," she smiled widely. "I just knew there was something going on between you two now."

"Yeah," Keera answered and offered Liam back to her best friend. Once the little one was safely tucked against his mother, Keera took Paddy's hand and faced her family.

"So – ehm – clearly, you all know now, but officially, Paddy and I are dating. We dated secretly about four years ago and then stopped when I went to college in America but we're dating again now, and things are… serious."

"Very serious," Paddy supplied. "I love Keera very much."

Everyone was quiet for a time then bursts of welcome and congratulations happened. Liam cried and everyone went quiet with a mumbled *sorry.*

"Tell us all about yourself," Deirdre took Paddy's arm and walked him over to the couch.

"Auntie, you've known him since he was a kid," Keera stated.

"Aye, well would you rather me ask when is the wedding?" Deirdre asked. Keera coughed as she nearly choked on air. "I thought not."

"Very soon if I have anything to say about it," Paddy winked, and the women squealed.

Keera's face went ashen, but she said nothing. Her eyes drifted to Ness, then Trish, they both married young, but as happy as Keera was for them, she didn't know if that was what she wanted. She knew she wanted Paddy, but marriage? A family? No. At least, not yet.

She was only twenty-three. There were things she wanted to do with her life. She wanted to travel. She wanted to write. She always wanted to be an author, though only four people knew that about her. She couldn't marry yet. She had so much more to do.

Sean's eyes were on her and when she looked over, he raised his brows in question. She tried to force a smile, but it failed. Before he could walk over to talk to her, the door opened, and Orin walked in holding the door for Emmet who looked pale and was breathing heavily. Cabhan walked in behind him, clearly trying not to look like he was hovering, but he was.

Emmet closed his eyes as pain rimmed his mouth and blew out a deep breath, almost as if he were blowing out a candle. Finally, he opened his eyes and looked around the room. Everyone stood frozen, unsure what to do and Keera knew

Emmet would hate that. He wouldn't want anyone walking on eggshells around him or treating him with kid-gloves. Things changed, he nearly died, but he wouldn't want the reminder.

"Hiya," he said.

"Can I get you anything, sweetheart?" Deirdre asked.

He shook his head. "Thanks, ma, but I'm not hungry. Where's Jacks?"

Almost as if he heard his name, Emmet's black lab barked and came out of the room they had made up for Emmet. His face brightened when he saw him and yet Keera saw tears gather in the corner of his eyes when he slowly bent to pet him.

"Hiya, lad," he said softly. Jacks sniffed him enthusiastically and looked up at him. His salt and pepper head tilting questioningly. Then, he whimpered. Emmet's back trembled and when he spoke, his voice was broken. "No, lad, I'm sorry," he said. "She's not with me. She isn't coming back."

Keera swallowed around the lump in her throat then looked around the room. Deirdre and Siobhan had tears in their eyes and the others looked away as if afraid they would start crying for him.

Jacks looked at Emmet for a long moment, huffed, and licked his chin. Keera couldn't see what was happening but Cabhan went to his brother when Emmet tried to straighten and couldn't.

"I'm going to lie down," Emmet said, not looking at his family. His father stood before him and nodded. Cabhan took a step holding Emmet's arm, lending support. "I can walk down a damn hallway by myself," he extracted his arm from his brother's grip.

Cabhan took a step back and raised his hands in peace. "I'll need to check on you frequently."

"I'm fine, dammit. I'm not a child."

"No, you're not," Cabhan agreed. "So, stop acting like

one."

"Go to hell," Emmet spat and walked down the hall snapping his fingers once for Jacks to follow.

Cabhan sighed and Deirdre went to her eldest stepson.

"Will he be all right?" she asked, dotting her eyes with Orin's handkerchief. Keera hadn't even seen her uncle hand his wife the folded piece of cotton.

Cabhan shrugged. "I don't know. He was better when Trevor was with him, but he fell asleep and Curtis took him back to the hotel. He insisted on walking from the car to the door alone and you saw what that did to him."

"He was as white as a sheet," Deirdre supplied.

"Aye," Cabhan replied. "Apart from the medical concerns with bullet wounds, he also has to deal with…" he cut off and glanced down the hallway.

"We understand, lad," Orin said. "But he has other reasons to live."

"Curtis and Joann will be bringing Trevor by in the morning. They extended their vacation for Emmet. Hopefully, when he's better, they'll talk about plans," Deirdre explained.

Cabhan shook his head. "He can't handle any added stress. I will need them to wait."

"They may not be able to, love," Deirdre said.

"Then we'll keep Trevor with us for a time," Orin stepped forward. "If they need to go back to America, he can be here."

"That's a wonderful idea, Orin," Siobhan stated. "I'd be happy to help too."

"Together we can figure it out," Deirdre nodded, smiling at Siobhan.

Keera's gaze moved to Paddy. His brows rose but she shook her head. Slipping down the hall when her Uncle Orin stepped into the restroom and no one but Paddy was watching her, she made her way to the closed door. Raising her fist to knock, she froze when she heard it. Sobs echoed behind the door, muffled as if into a pillow but sobs, nonetheless. Jacks whimpered but the crying didn't stop.

Keera pressed her trembling lips together as tears formed in her eyes. Emmet was hurt, deeply hurt and there was nothing she could do about it. Except be there for him. Knowing he wouldn't want anyone to hear him, she wiped her tears when she heard him cry out louder and a dull thud sounding like he punched the pillow or mattress.

Turning away, she headed back down the long hallway, seeing Paddy coming toward her. His eyes twitched when he saw her tears, but he opened his arms to her, and she gratefully stepped into them. He wrapped her in his embrace and held her tightly.

"Shh, it's all right. He'll be all right," he soothed. Keera nodded into his chest and pulled back. "Do you want to go out there and have dinner?" he asked, indicating the main room.

She nodded, hoping he wouldn't bring up how she froze earlier when the *m-word* was mentioned. Fortunately, he didn't, and she breathed a little easier. Before they entered the main room, he stopped her and turned her to him.

"Keera O'Quinn," he said, and her stomach flipped, landing near her feet. Her mouth instantly went dry and her hands felt clammy. Black speckles entered her vision as he took her hands. "Will you... go out to dinner with me tomorrow night?"

Keera gave a long low moan and swayed. "Dear god, don't do that!" she smacked his arm. "I thought you were proposing."

Paddy chuckled. "How romantic of me," he winked. "Asking you to marry me in the hallway of my best friend's parent's house while he's down the hall mourning the loss of his wife. I'm not that heartless, love. And besides, I saw your reaction when it was brought up. But I don't want to talk about that right now. So, will you go to dinner with me?"

"Yes," she smiled. "I would love to."

"Good. I'll pick you up here at six tomorrow?"

"Five forty-five," she corrected. "I want a good snog before we go anywhere."

"Only fifteen minutes for a snog?" Paddy laughed. "Aye, all right. Five forty-five it is. But don't think that will only happen *before* dinner."

Keera's lips and body tingled. "I am looking forward to it."

"Oh, so am I," he took her hand and kissed it.

Chapter Eleven

Seeing Keera holding a baby caused something very caveman-like to rear its head inside him. But her nearly death-like paleness at the mention of marriage cooled that flame. Granted, Paddy knew she was young and probably didn't want to marry yet, but he was approaching thirty-three and he had set his sights on only one. The evening, apart from Emmet's sadness had gone well. Better than he expected. Emmet hadn't emerged from the room before Paddy left and he hoped his friend would still want to talk to him later. Knowing it wasn't a good time, Paddy waited. Emmet had come around with Keera. He was sure he could come around with him, too. In time.

As he stood in his bathroom, tying a tie for his date with Keera, his phone rang.

Uncle Tully.

Answering it, he put it on speaker.

"Hiya, Uncle Tully," he said.

"Heya, lad, how goes it?"

"Not too bad," he answered. "Heading out on a date here in the next fifteen minutes."

"Oh, aye? And who's the lucky lady?"

"Actually, Keera has given me another chance."

"Keera? Really?" He heard the hesitation in his uncle's voice.

"You don't have to sound so shocked," Paddy chuckled.

"No, no, of course not. It's just, I remember what happened fifteen months ago and even before that. I just want to make sure you're all right... you're prepared."

"I know and I am. A lot has happened this last week, but I'll tell you all about it later. When are you back in Limerick?"

"Flight leaves in two hours," he said.

"Sorry to say goodbye to London?" Paddy asked, grateful his uncle dropped the topic of his past with Keera.

"Hell no," he laughed. "But it's been good to me."

"Good, need me to pick you up?"

"What, and ruin your night?" He heard the suggestive tone in his uncle's voice and chuckled.

"I don't think *that's* going to happen tonight."

"Why not?"

"Well, a lot of reasons but mainly, tonight is about reconnecting."

"Reconnecting... might want to rethink your words," his uncle laughed.

"Yeah yeah," Paddy waved it off. "But hey, when you're back, I'd like to come see you."

"Of course, anytime, lad, you know I'd love that."

"And I'd like to bring Keera."

His uncle paused for a moment. "Even better," he finally replied.

"She really means a lot to me, Uncle Tully."

"I know that, lad. I just don't like how she's hurt you."

"We've hurt each other. We've talked and we can't deny our feelings for each other. This is the real deal."

"Then I'm happy for you. I would love to meet her. But I can't promise not to remember all that's happened."

"I know and I don't expect you to just forget. But, please give her a chance? She's amazing and I... love her."

Tully was quiet. "She won't break your heart again?"

"I can't promise we won't have our ups and downs. I can't promise we won't hurt each other. But we've agreed to always communicate with each other and talk it out. I'm happy where we are. Really."

"All right, I'll give her a clean slate. But just know, if she hurts you again... without provocation, I will not be so kind."

"I know," Paddy grinned. He knew exactly what his uncle did to people he didn't like.

"I have an event on the nineteenth. How about you come then?"

"That'd be perfect. See you then."

"All right, lad, I'll text you when I land. Have fun tonight and don't do anything I wouldn't do."

"At least that gives me options," Paddy teased, and his uncle chuckled.

"Oh, they're calling me to the car, I gotta go, lad."

"Bye, Uncle Tully, see you in a week, aye?"

"Aye, lad, see you then! I love you," he signed off.

"Love you too." Paddy loved hearing those words.

His uncle was his mother's brother and raised him when his parents died. He put his own career on hold to raise an eleven-year-old. Having been a bachelor and then raising a young kid who felt like an outcast from his own family, Uncle Tully always told him and showed how much he cared. Paddy wanted for nothing and Tully did everything in his power to help him. After Paddy reached eighteen, they became more like best friends than uncle and nephew.

The alarm he set rang and, after silencing it, he pocked his phone, wallet, and keys and made his way to his car. Fortunately, he remembered the flowers he had the florist make up and put into a vase.

Making his way to Keera's aunt's and uncle's house where she and her mom were staying to help with Emmet, he wondered how the night would go and how to ask her to go with him to Limerick in a week.

All thought aside, he pulled up to the house and nearly froze. Emmet stood outside, letting his dog out but what shocked Paddy even more was he held a lit cigarette between his fingers. Emmet hadn't smoked since he was at Uni and had strongly encouraged everyone in his circle of family and friends to not smoke after he had realized the health implications. But even though Paddy was surprised, he couldn't fault him. He'd been through hell.

Slowing the car, he took a deep breath before parking, grabbing the flowers, and getting out. Emmet watched him and tossed the cigarette down, squashing it with his foot.

"Heya," Paddy started.

"Hey," Emmet answered.

"I won't ask how you are doing because I'm sure you're sick of hearing that. So, I'll just say, you look better."

"Yeah, a bit," he replied.

"I'm glad."

They were quiet and Paddy refused to allow his nerves to surface. He stood still, even if he wanted to shift from foot to foot. When the silence lingered, Paddy decided to come clean.

"Look, Em, I'm sorry. I'm sorry I went behind your back, and I'm sorry I never told you. But you have to understand, I love your cousin more than anything and I want to spend the rest of my life with her. I know, not telling you how I felt was wrong and I'm sorry. I know what you know about me and honestly looking at it from where you're standing, I get it. But... it's not like that with her. I love her, man and that's not going away."

Emmet took a deep breath, still not looking at him, his eyes were on Jacks sniffing around a couple flowers.

"Jacks," Emmet called then whistled. The dog looked up. "Not in ma's flowers." The old dog trotted around to a tree instead. "I'm not going to sugarcoat anything, Paddy. I hate the thought of you with Keera. You are not who I hoped for her. She deserves someone who isn't like... you. She deserves someone who won't even look at another woman when with her. And quite frankly, she deserves someone younger. The fact you kept it a secret, tells me you were ashamed of her and knew how it would be and how I'd feel. I'm not happy with this."

"I am not ashamed of her or being with her or my actions. I love her."

"Good to know," Emmet scoffed. Then huffed a sigh. "She has told me she loves you and has asked me to give you another chance. I'm hesitant, I admit. Love is not something I believe in, anymore. She's like a sister to me. It was wrong of me to fire you. I wasn't in my right mind. You're welcome to keep working for me, if you want. And I will... try to wrap my head around this and attempt to accept it for both your sakes. You've been a good friend, Paddy. My best friend for many years. I am just surprised at how you haven't told me. How *she* hasn't told me. Understand where I'm coming from."

"I do and I take full responsibility," Paddy answered. "I can't excuse the past, all I can say is, everything I've done, everything I do, is for her. I love her."

"I can see that since she told me it was her decision not to tell anyone and you took the blame. It makes me realize how much you truly care," Emmet again huffed a sigh and Paddy thought, for the briefest moment, about telling him he had been to see Mara but decided against it. "Anyway, you hurt her, and I'll make every one of your phobias, fears, and worst nightmares come to life, clear?"

"Chrystal," he answered.

Emmet gave another loud whistle and told Jacks to come. The dog ambled over to him.

"For a moment there, I thought I'd be getting a black eye," Paddy laughed.

"Trust me, I thought about it but realized I'd probably hurt myself more than you and decided against it."

"Appreciate it," he said.

They both walked to the door and Emmet let him in. Keera stood in the middle of the room, a nervous look all over her face. Her mother sat on the couch and her aunt in the chair.

"Are you all right?" she went over to him.

"Perfectly fine, thanks," Emmet answered.

She threw him a look and then gazed back at Paddy.

"Fine, love," he answered handing her the flowers. "We just had a talk. You ready?"

"These are beautiful," she gasped. Then looked back at her mom and aunt. Siobhan stepped forward and offered to take the vase of roses.

"I won't keep her out too late," Paddy said nodding to both women.

"Have fun," Siobhan called as they left.

Keera followed him to his car. He helped her in, then jogged around to the other side. Sliding into the seat, he didn't turn on the car, he leaned over, grasped the back of her neck and kissed her slowly and thoroughly. When he pulled back, she had a grin a mile long.

"Missed you too," she said.

"You have no idea, baby," he sat back in his seat and started the car up.

"That's it?" she questioned. He threw her his trademark smirk.

"Not even close, but I didn't think it would be best to give anyone a show," he pointed to the window and Keera caught the quick movements of her mom and aunt as they hid behind the see-through curtain. She giggled.

"I swear, it's like they have no shame," she teased.

"None, love," he answered. "But I have some decorum. We'll find some hidden place and I'll give you what you beg for."

"Beg?" she questioned. "Since when have I ever begged?"

"Since today," he winked and put the car into gear, driving away from the house.

Chapter Twelve

Keera couldn't keep the giddy feeling hidden. She had seen several nice locations where he could have pulled off, but Paddy kept driving. When she heard him pull up to the house and knew Emmet was outside still letting Jacks out, her nerves took over and she paced. As soon as Paddy came in, she had searched his body for any sign of discomfort or bruising but saw none. She only hoped that meant Emmet was coming around to them as a couple.

But they were alone then, and she was excited, not only to kiss Paddy again, which was one of her favorite things to do, but to also have dinner with him. Knowing Paddy, it was somewhere nice.

She looked down at her black short skater dress and

hoped it was fancy enough. Where he got the money to take her to five-star Michelin restaurants and order the most expensive wine, she never knew but Paddy never disappointed. And sure enough, when he pulled up to Tabby's, she smiled. But when they got out of the car, she read the times of operation on the side window and her excitement dimmed.

"Paddy, they're closed today," she said.

"Hmm," he locked the car and walked over to her. "Good thing I rented the whole place and am friends with the chef."

He knocked twice followed by once on the door and it opened to a man dressed in a white chef's coat and black slacks.

"Paddy," he smiled.

"Marco," Paddy answered. "This is Miss O'Quinn."

"Ah, *que bella*," he said looking at her. "Come in, come in."

Paddy motioned for her to go in ahead of him and she gasped. The restaurant was exquisite; brick, stone, timber, chandeliers, and wrought iron all meshed to make the exclusive restaurant look inviting and elegant in a homey way. She followed Marco toward the back near the brick enclosed wine cellar. He gestured to a table for two, covered in white linen. Paddy took Marco's hand in a shake and pulled him into a hug.

"Grand, cheers, Marco, this is fantastic."

"*Va bene,*" he answered. Paddy sat and Marco gestured for a young man to come forward. "Now, my son Marco Junior will take care of you. I will say we got in some wonderful fresh oysters today and I have been smoking the salmon all day. It's–" he kissed his fingers. "Delicious. Now, I leave you in Marco's capable hands."

"Thanks, pop," Marco Junior said as Chef Marco walked back toward the kitchen. "Please call me Marc. The champagne you ordered has been on ice, would you like to start with that or a bottle of wine?"

"I think champagne," Paddy looked at her. "That all right?"

"Perfect, thank you," she answered.

"And we'll start with the smoked salmon," Paddy said to Marco then turned back to Keera. "Would you like to try the oysters?" She shrugged, not knowing if she would like them or not. Her mother didn't, so she had never had them. "We'll have the smoked salmon and the seafood cocktail instead, Marc."

"An excellent choice," he said. "I'll put the order in for pop and get your champagne."

"Cheers thanks."

Paddy turned to her and smiled. "You all right?"

"You rented this entire place? Just for me?" she blurted. "On a Friday night?"

"Of course," then he stopped. "Is that all right?"

"Yeah," she assured. "It's just a bit overwhelming. I'm used to a chipy and beer."

"Not with me and not now we're official," he took her hand in his. "I hope it's not too much for you."

She leaned in and lowered her voice. "How much is all of this?" she questioned. "It can't be cheap."

"I don't want you worrying about that, it's already taken care of," he stated giving her hand a gentle squeeze. "And I want you to enjoy yourself and get whatever you want, all right?"

Keera took a deep breath and let it out quickly. *What the hell,* she thought.

"Okay, thank you. This is amazing."

Paddy winked and leaned back as Marc came up with the bottle of champagne he ordered.

Chapter Thirteen

Five courses and three bottles of champagne later, Keera was walking on air. Paddy had kept his promise of kissing her languidly, thoroughly, and in that toe-curling way only he could. In between each course, he would take his time showing her how much he loved her.

Though they drank heavily, they paced themselves and had plenty of water. Keera wanted to remember every detail of that evening.

When they said goodbye, thanking both Marcos for everything, it was a little sad. She loved the evening so much. She didn't want it to end. But as she and Paddy walked along High Street, hand in hand, her heart soared with so much emotion she let out a nervous giggle.

Paddy looked down at her and chuckled. "What was that for?" he asked.

"This evening," she sighed happily, resting her head on his bicep. "I don't want it to end."

"I know. I don't either," he said.

They walked in silence, taking in the evening hustle and bustle. Finally, Paddy spoke again.

"How would you feel if I told you, I got tickets to see TS Jameson at his latest event in Limerick next weekend?" She froze, gaping at him. "Would you want to go with me?"

The giddy feeling grew in the pit of her stomach and she grinned. "Go with you?" she screeched. "Yes! My god, yes! I've always wanted to meet him. Oh my god, oh my god," she felt almost faint as she threw her arms around his neck and squeezed.

Paddy chuckled, holding her tightly to him and burying his face in her neck.

"Bastard! Get your hands off my girlfriend!" she heard, then felt Paddy be ripped away from her.

It all happened so quickly. Paddy heard someone shout something about a girlfriend and then he was being yanked around and pain exploded across his jaw, radiating up his cheek and toward his eyes. Someone had punched him. Hard. Growling, Paddy righted himself, happy to say he stayed on his feet. Turning, he saw a man, more like a boy, he recognized him as he had seen him only briefly fifteen months ago when he followed Keera after their moment in the alleyway. The boy clenched his fists ready to attack again. This time, Paddy was ready for him. Sidestepping his sloppy right hook, Paddy jabbed the boy's side, a direct hit to his kidneys. The boy cried out and doubled over giving Paddy the perfect opening. Another hit to his gut had the boy gasping for air.

"Stop!" Keera shrieked. Paddy looked over at her, her face was pale as she watched the scene unfold. Paddy released the boy with a shove and watched as he stumbled back.

"You know this jackanapes?" Paddy demanded; his jaw still hurt but fortunately nothing felt broken.

"He's my boyfriend," she said.

Every fiber of Paddy's body bristled at that word. "What?"

"I—I mean, he *was,*" she stammered.

Paddy's hands shook and the hair on the back of his neck stood on end.

"We're over," Keera stated.

"No, babe, we agreed a break, but I still want you back," the boy said from the ground.

"Tell me what's going on," Paddy growled.

"Don't use that tone with me," Keera snapped.

"If you've been using me as a distraction until you're ready to take him back then yeah, I think I have every right to use any *tone* I damn well want to use. Is it true you are only on a break? That you planned on getting back together with him?"

"No!" Keera shouted. "This time was different."

"*This* time?" Paddy's blood boiled. "How many *breaks* have you two been on?"

Keera looked at him. He didn't know what he looked like, but he could imagine. Feral was almost too kind a word. He couldn't believe history was repeating.

"Paddy, please," she started.

"Unbelievable," he shook his head and, with a look back at the boy on the ground, he shrugged. "All yours." As he walked away, he stopped himself from looking back.

"Paddy!" Keera cried. He turned then to see the look in

her eyes. Hurt, confusion, anger, maybe that last was his reflection, he wasn't sure.

"If, and it's obviously a big if, you are ever done with him, find me. But until then, don't come near me."

"Wait just a minute," she stomped her food.

"No, you lied to me and I was fool enough to believe you."

"Just stop, okay," she shouted. "Patrick," she looked at the boy finally getting on his feet. "We are over. We have been since you told me we needed a break. I told you I was done then, but you don't understand that. Let me spell it out for you... we are over. I'm not your girlfriend. I haven't been for three months."

"But babe, I told you—"

"No," she cut him off. "Enough. I cared for you when we were together but now, I'm over the *are we-aren't we* shite and I'm ready to be with the person I have always loved. I'm sorry, but that's not you. Goodbye, Patrick."

"You can't be serious," the boy said.

Keera shrugged, her eyes on Paddy. "I've loved him since I was eighteen. I'm sorry, Patrick."

Patrick's eyes went from Keera to Paddy then back. "This isn't over," he stated. "We're not done."

"Yes, we are," she declared. "Move on, Patrick."

She looked back toward Paddy, her eyes filling with question. He knew then, he could never stay angry at her. The boy, as Paddy dubbed him, huffed a sigh and walked away mumbling something to himself. Keera never dropped Paddy's gaze as she walked slowly over to him.

"I'm sorry I didn't tell you about Patrick. Honestly, I never thought it'd be a problem. I never thought *he* would be a problem. Last time I told him we were done but he didn't realize it, I guess. Are *we* okay?"

Paddy took a deep breath. His sudden urge to walk

away, tempered. She was not Stephanie, he had to remind himself. Keera's shoulders slumped when he didn't answer.

"I guess not... Could you take me home, please?" she asked softly.

He wanted to talk to her, tell her why he behaved like he did. Tell her she wasn't alone. He's messed up worse than that and other he knew intimately had been even worse. But it all died on his lips. He couldn't say the words. She turned on her heels and he could do nothing but follow her to the car.

Keera successfully held back the tears as Paddy drove. The most beautiful sunset drifted over Lough Leane, the water shimmering like crystals. That was not how she expected to end the night with Paddy, but he had shown how he felt about Patrick and her silence regarding their relationship. Truthfully, she had thought this breakup with Patrick O'Flannery would be the last. She didn't love him, not at all. She like the bad boy, always had but love was most definitely not in the equation. Not like it was with Paddy.

When her aunt's and uncle's house came into view, she was sure her tightly held tears would leak but again, she surprised herself with her strength. She would lose it as soon as the door shut, she knew, but until then...

She unbuckled her seatbelt, not looking in Paddy's direction. When he still hadn't said anything or made a move to walk her to the door, she spoke low to keep the emotion from her tone.

"Thank you for a wonderful dinner," she said. "I enjoyed every second of it and though I know you probably never want to see me or do this again, I swear to you, I told you the truth. I love you, Paddy O'Shea and I never thought the man I considered my ex would sway you into thinking I ever lied to you. I'm sorry our beautiful evening ended like this."

She couldn't stop herself. She leaned over the console and kissed his bruising jaw. The brownish red stubble hid the extent of his injuries. Again, he said nothing and made no move to do anything. Keera held back her tears and opened the car door. She didn't look back when she reached the front door, she couldn't. Her tears already threatened to fall, and she refused to be looked at as weak. When she heard the creaking pop of the gravel beneath the tires, she knew he was leaving and something inside her broke.

A strangled wail left her lips and she crumpled to the front stoop. She wept harder than she ever had before. The door opened and her mom, uncle, and aunt stood there.

"Keera?" Her mom questioned and crouched down, wrapping her arms around her. "What's wrong, sweetie?"

Keera cried harder. Her aunt and uncle were talking, and it sounded like Emmet had joined them. She was too heartbroken to feel embarrassed. But when her mom's soothing voice finally broke through her haze, she pulled back and locked eyes with her.

"Oh ma'," she cried. "He's so angry with me and I-"

"Who is, honey?" her aunt questioned.

"Paddy."

"Did he hurt you?" Emmet demanded.

She shook her head. "It was so amazing, wonderful... and then..."

"What, sweetie?" her mom asked.

Keera finally got control of her emotions, took a deep breath, and launched into the story of Patrick attacking Paddy and how Paddy's entire demeanor changed. She told them of the silent car ride home and how he hadn't done anything. She told them about how she apologized and told him how much he meant to her. All of it came pouring out.

They all crowded around her as she stayed on the stoop

in her mother's arms.

"I just don't understand what went wrong." She wiped her eyes. "I was so sorry, but I honestly thought we were over. Am I to suffer because of another's thoughts? Patrick clearly didn't think the same as me but how is that my fault?"

"It's not, honey," her mother said.

"Well, he clearly thinks it is," she replied.

"I wonder..." her uncle began. "And this is in no way defending him, if you want him out of your life, I'll grab my shovel," she couldn't help the laugh that burst forth. "But sweetie, maybe there's something we don't know about. Something he went through that made this seem much more... I don't know, more than it should have been."

All eyes turned to Emmet, who shrugged. "Don't look at me," he answered. "He kept your relationship a secret, he can keep others. But I'm with da'. I'll kill him if you want. The bastard. I told him not to hurt you."

Keera felt the tears linger in her eyes. She didn't want Paddy hurt. Everyone stayed silent as Keera processed everything that happened. She sighed heavily and rubbed her hands on her knees.

"Well," she said. "I guess... I should—"

She was cut off by the sound of tires on gravel. Her eyes snapped up to see Paddy's car pulling back up. The darkness around them infiltrated the car and she couldn't see his face. She held her breath and when he didn't get out quickly, she heard Emmet growl and take a step down, but his father stopped him.

"Let's go back inside," Orin said.

"But da'," Emmet argued.

"Now, Em," he stated. Emmet grumbled but she felt the heat behind her leave and her mom kissed her temple.

"You don't have to do or listen to anything you don't want to," Siobhan said. "We are right behind the door."

Keera took a deep breath and let it out slowly. "I know."

"You're not alone, sweetheart," Orin said. "Just say the word."

Keera nodded and looked back at the car. Once, when she was alone, she counted to twenty and the driver's side door opened.

Chapter

Fourteen

"Dammit!" Paddy shouted as he struck the steering wheel. He had only made it to the end of the driveway. The car idled as he stared out to the darkness, his headlights the only beam of light around. He had done what he didn't want to do. He had put his history on Keera, and he felt sick. She didn't deserve it. Stephanie deliberately manipulated him, Keera never would. That Patrick O'Flannery was bad news but all he could see was the ugly truth when he learned about Stephanie's betrayal. Taking a deep breath, he pulled out his phone but knew she deserved an in-person apology. Looking behind him, he put the car into reverse, and pulled into the grass to turn the car around. It was tight but he would make it work. He had to. Keera meant everything to him.

He put the car in park when the front door came into

view, but with it, Keera's mom, aunt and uncle, and of course – he swallowed audibly – Emmet. Reminding himself that his friend was hurt and would probably not be able to do much more than punch him, his jaw ached from the boy's punch earlier that day.

Siobhan kissed Keera's cheek and in the glow of his headlights, he saw tear tracks on her beautiful face, and he hated himself all over again. Everyone left the stoop and Keera was alone. Again, taking a deep breath, he turned off the car, wondering for a brief moment if he should have left it running in case Emmet returned with a hunting rifle. Pocketing the keys and popping the door open, Paddy got out.

Keera stood, wringing her hands in front of her and scrunching her nose in the way he adored. How he would have ruined the most perfect evening over some inconsequential thing like a jealous *ex*-boyfriend, he didn't understand.

"Kee," he started on a harsh sigh. "I'm so sorry."

She took a shaky breath and nodded quickly but if he expected her to run into his arms, she didn't.

"What happened, Paddy? We promised each other we would be open and honest. I didn't tell you about Patrick because I thought we were over. Honestly, this *break* wasn't like all the others. I told him I was done. He obviously thought I wasn't serious. After the scare with the baby... I realized, stronger than ever, I want to be with you and no one else. I thought I made that clear."

"You did," he huffed and thrust his hands into his hair. "Can we sit?"

She stared into his eyes for a long moment but eventually nodded and sat back on the stoop, scooting to the end. Paddy sat beside her and rested his elbows on his knees.

"I was engaged," he admitted. She looked over at him.

"When?"

"While you were in American," he replied and saw the

shock on her face. "It was a whirlwind thing. When you stopped taking my calls and that last conversation, we had about seeing other people... well, I met Stephanie. She was completely different than you. She was everything I thought I wanted. I wanted you but was angry because I had held out for you and when you said you wanted to see other people, I sort of lost it. Fell back on my player reputation but honestly, it was never what I wanted. I met Stephanie when she and her friends checked into the Plaza for a Hen Party. I stuck around after work at the bar where I knew they were drinking. She invited me to drink with them. We all got very drunk and she slipped her hotel room key into my hand. I'll spare you the details.

We dated for about two months and I decided *what the hell.* I bought a ring and asked her to marry me. She said yes and we planned on going to the courthouse at the end of the week. She never... well, that day when the judge asked if anyone objected, the door opened, and a man walked in. He said he objected because Stephanie was his wife of seven years and had been gone for two months on a *soul-searching* journey. One of her friends at the Hen Party had told the man of her... indiscretions. She had never told me she was married, nor that she had ever been. The man punched me, nearly broke my jaw and gave me a black eye. I was so stunned I couldn't defend myself. The man demanded a divorce and she ran after him crying, saying I had forced her to marry or I would have told him. Total shite, but I was summoned to the Garda to give a statement. It was embarrassing and I honestly thought I was going to be arrested.

Fortunately, the husband dropped the charges when it was revealed I wasn't the only one and in fact she had a husband before the one who objected. That whole situation made me leery and honestly, hesitant. I didn't date anyone after Stephanie until you and—"

"And here Patrick O'Flannery claimed I was still dating him. Oh, Paddy, I'm so sorry." She grasped his forearm.

"I rubber banded," he admitted. "I reverted back to Stephanie. Even though I knew it was you and not her, I still felt betrayed."

"I understand," Keera nodded. "I'm sorry that happened to you. And I'm sorry for not telling you but I didn't think I needed to. To me, he was in the past."

"It's not your fault. We both had a life and we've both kept things from each other. But I swear to you, today, our wonderful date, I love you and only you, Keera O'Quinn. And I will not take you for granted. I will always tell you how I am feeling. I'm committed to you, us, this," he took her hand in his and angled to look her in the eye. "Can you forgive me for being an arse?"

She giggled and wiped her cheeks. "Yes," she nodded. "I can, Paddy O'Shea. I love you and I am committed to us too."

Paddy framed her face and leaned toward her. She closed the distance, threw her arms around his neck and kissed him deeper than he had felt before, patching up the pieces of his life and heart.

When she finally pulled back, her grin stretched across her face. *So lovely.*

"Do I still get to go with you to Limerick?"

"Oh, of course," he replied, confident his grin was just as wide as hers.

"Oh good," she sighed in relief. "I *really* wanted to meet TS Jameson."

Paddy chuckled. "That's all I'm good for, huh? Meeting facilitation."

"Not true…" she stated then bit her lower lip. "You also make a great chauffer."

Paddy threw his head back and laughed. Pulled her closer to him, he kissed her once more.

"Then, your highness, I'll pick you up at four on Friday," he said.

"I'll be ready," she answered. "Where will we be

staying?"

"I have family in the area," he explained.

"You do?" she questioned.

"Yeah, my Uncle Tully will put us up," he said.

"Oh," she shrugged. "You never talked about him."

"He's the uncle who took me in after my parents were killed."

"Oh! That uncle!" she exclaimed. "Sorry, I didn't think you mentioned his name before."

"Yeah, he's the only uncle I talk to."

"Do you think..." she looked away.

"What?" he asked gently.

"Do you think he'd be okay if we... shared a room?"

Paddy stared at her for along moment, then a slow grin spread across his lips. "I think he would think there was something wrong with me if we didn't."

"Good," she breathed out. "Because I miss you."

"Never again, love," he said. "You won't ever have to miss me again."

He leaned forward and captured her lips once more.

"Now, do you have everything, love?" Siobhan asked Keera for the third time. Having decided to head home to Siobhan's and Keera's home in County Clare as it was closer to Limerick, Keera packed a small bag and then fell onto her bed near where her mom sat. A grin broke across her face and she looked over.

"Yes," she said.

"Oh, honey! I'm so excited for you! Just promise me,

you'll be careful." Her meaning was clear.

"We will," Keera confirmed. "Paddy and I talked. We don't want another scare. He's... stocking up."

Her mom giggled like a schoolgirl. "I can't believe you get to meet TS Jameson! I wouldn't mind meeting him for the evening. So handsome!"

"Ma," Keera made a face. "Gross and isn't he like, way older than you?" Siobhan raised an eyebrow. "Yeah yeah," she waved her off considering Paddy was a good ten years older than she was.

"This is a dream come true for you, love," Siobhan began. "Meeting the author who inspired you to start writing all while on the arm of the man you love. I want you to have fun, but always remember who you are."

Keera nodded and they both looked toward the hallway as Paddy knocked. Siobhan stood to open the door. Keera's smile refused to leave as she saw Paddy come in and lock eyes with her. His slow perusal made her skin itch and tingle. As excited as she was to meet TS Jameson, she couldn't decide if she was more excited to be with Paddy again.

"You look amazing," he whispered. She grinned and waited expectantly as he walked in and slipped his arm around her waist. Teasingly, he finally captured her lips with his. "Are you ready?" he asked.

She nodded. "Can't wait," winking, she gripped his arse making him grunt and chuckle.

"Down girl," he whispered and threw a look toward her mother, who was smiling but not looking their way. "Let's go," he said. "We should be there early. My uncle apologizes, he will be out tonight, but we'll meet up for dinner. I went ahead and got us a hotel for the next couple nights just in case..." he dropped his voice. "I remember how loud you get. Didn't want to give Uncle Tully a show."

She pretended indignation and playfully slapped his

arm even as her eyes twinkled.

"And… when do we meet TS Jameson?"

"What… booted out for a sixty-five-year-old man with an overactive imagination? Don't know if I should be hurt or prove you wrong."

"Prove me wrong," she whispered and clasped the back of his neck pulling him down to her.

He kissed her, making her toes curl inside her sketchers and the hair on her arms stand up. Her mother cleared her throat softly. They broke apart and Keera looked down, her cheeks heating.

"You had better get going, loves," Siobhan stated. "There's a storm coming."

"Ms. O'Quinn, thank you for supporting us."

Siobhan looked over at him. "Paddy, I see how happy you make my daughter."

"I wanted to apologize again for the issue the other day. I hope you know how much Keera means to me."

"Nothing to apologize for, Keera explained everything. We've all made mistakes but don't hurt her like that again and you and I will have nothing to worry about. But if she cries to me like that again, Emmet isn't the only one you'll need to worry about, understood?"

Paddy nodded. "Yes, ma'am."

"Good, then you should start calling me Siobhan."

"Siobhan," Paddy agreed. "Though it feels a little odd."

"You'll get used to it," she winked. "Now, off you go. Be careful and, Kee, let me know when you get there, okay?"

"I will, ma," she hugged her mom while Paddy grabbed her suitcase. "Love you."

"Love you too," she kissed her cheek.

They walked to Paddy's car and after securing her suitcase next to his duffle, he opened the door for her, and Keera waved to her mom standing in the doorway. Paddy slid into the driver's side. Once on the road, he turned to her.

"Ready to meet TS Jameson, love?" he asked.

"More than ready. I can't wait. You know, he inspired me to start writing."

"Writing? You? You write? How did I not know this?"

"I don't tell many people."

"Yeah, but I'm not most people," he grinned. "It's fantastic! What do you write?"

She shrugged. "It's mainly scribbles, ideas, nothing concrete."

"Can I see them?" he asked.

She looked at his profile as the Irish Countryside sped past. "I've only shared them with four people; ma, Uncle Orin, Aunt Dee, and Emmet."

"I'd love to see them. Maybe you can share them with my– with TS Jameson when we see him."

"Oh god no!" she looked horrified.

"Why not?"

"Because, he's… him… a great author. I'm nobody."

"You are *not* nobody," Paddy stated and took her hand in his. "And I've heard he enjoys mentoring young authors. He's said, he's not going to live forever so it would be nice to encourage new authors."

"You've heard, huh?" she questioned. "How have you heard?"

"Oh, you know, interviews."

"Hmm, I know you're hiding something, O'Shea. What and why, I don't know.

He winked at her. "If I am, know it's all in good fun."

"I have ways to get the truth out of you," she turned to look at him and grinned when he squirmed.

"We'll be there in thirty minutes; can you wait to jump me until then?" he asked.

"I'll try," she giggled.

Chapter Fifteen

Paddy pressed his foot down a little more on the pedal. The sooner he got to Limerick, the sooner he could have Keera the way he truly wanted. She still affected him. He was positive she always would. He couldn't wait to introduce her to his Uncle Tully. He would love her.

Glancing over at her, she was looking through his phone's music app for the next song. The sunlight broke through the clouds at that moment and her hair glistened like strands of gold. He smiled in disbelief. It had been five years since he first laid eyes on her and even then, she stole his breath.

She cried eureka and played a song. The pop song was one he had never heard.

"That's not on my music..." he said.

"Nope, I found it on the streaming app you have," she announced. "It's a bit old but still the perfect road trip song," she said and proceeded to sing along.

He chuckled as he watched her put her hands up as the song said and sing at the top of her lungs. A sense of contentment surrounded him. He was happy.

The drive to Limerick was easy and fun. Keera was happy none of the awkwardness from the weekend had travelled with them. When they pulled off the highway, Keera turned down the music so he could concentrate more. It was eerily quiet when his phone rang in her hand. She squealed but looked down. On the screen there was a picture of two men, one she recognized as Paddy and the other was an older man with shoulder length silvery brown hair, a medium length light grey beard and the deepest brown eyes she had ever seen. In the picture, they were both laughing as they looked at the camera, arms slung around each other, glasses of whiskey in hand. Both wore a suit jacket with their button up shirts open at the collar. The contact name was *Uncle Tully*.

"Are you going to answer that?" Paddy questioned.

"Oh, sorry, sure." She slid the bar over and put the phone to her ear. "Paddy O'Shea's phone, Keera speaking."

"Well, now I know what he meant," an older man's voice began on the other end of the phone.

"I'm sorry?"

"He said your voice was smooth as silk. I can understand. I've never heard a smoother sound in all my sixty-five years."

Keera giggled nervously. "Put him on speaker," Paddy said. She did. "Try not to steal my woman before you've even met her, Uncle Tully."

"Just letting her know she has options," Keera could hear

the tease in his voice.

"Yeah, sure," Paddy chuckled. "We're about ten minutes out from the house. I did book us a room at the Pier Hotel. We'll check in there first."

"Still don't know why you wasted the money, son. I sleep with earplugs so I wouldn't have heard anything, if you know what I mean."

Keera felt her cheeks heat.

"Yeah, yeah," Paddy waved him off. "We still on for dinner after... we meet TS Jameson?"

"Sure, of course. I made reservations. I'll meet you there at eight," Tully said.

"Yeah, definitely, unless you need me to help with anything?" Paddy offered.

"Nah, I got it, lad. You check in. I'll see you later. I am looking forward to meeting you, Miss O'Quinn."

"You too, Mister..." she realized she didn't know his last name. Paddy had told her Uncle Tully was his mother's brother. "Sir." She went with the standard title.

"Ooh, lass, don't be calling me that, might give me delusions of grandeur. Just Tully will work for me."

"Tully," she smiled.

"Enjoy the book signing and I will have some wine at our table," Tully offered. "Red or white?"

"Sounds great, see you soon! And either is fine," Paddy called.

"Lass?" Tully asked.

"Red sounds wonderful, thank you," Keera answered. "If that's okay with you."

"Of course, see you both soon," Tully signed off and Keera hung up the phone.

"Where is your uncle going to be tonight?" she asked.

"He works at Limerick University. They're having a reception for a travelling author."

"Jameson?"

"Hmm? Oh, no, some former student who wrote some dissertation on the water causeway of Pompeii or something or other. He said he would much rather be with us, but he's a tenured professor, he has to be there."

"What does he teach?" she asked.

"He's in the English department. Now, could you help me look? I always miss my turn up here."

Chapter Sixteen

After checking in at the hotel, Paddy and Keera headed up to their room. The view from the floor to ceiling window was spectacular. Overlooking the River Shannon, King John's Castle, and the Sarsfield Bridge.

Paddy walked up behind her and wrapped his arms around her waist, resting his chin on her shoulder.

"We have some time before the event. Do you want a glass of wine or a beer?" he asked.

She leaned back into him and smiled. "You made me promise not to jump you until we made it to the hotel and now you ask if I want a drink?" She turned in his arms, wrapping hers around his neck. "Are you nervous, O'Shea?"

Paddy let out a breathy chuckle. "No," but his eyes

proved he was lying.

With a slight smirk, Keera pulled back slightly and pushed on his chest. He let his momentum carry him backwards and bounced as he landed on the bed. Looking up at her, his throat closed, and his mouth dried instantly as she pulled her t-shirt over her head.

"Damn," he muttered. She wore the sheer lacey bra he loved so much. Her grin stole his breath. She enjoyed his perusal.

The mattress bowed as she knelt, straddling his hips. "I was just thinking..." he muttered as she began unbuttoning his shirt.

"That's the problem," she stated.

"Wh-what is?" he gasped as she slid her hands up his bare chest.

"You thinking," she answered leaning down to suck his collarbone. "Don't think."

"Shite," he cursed and placed his hands on her hips. Twisting, he hovered over her and duplicated her actions. Looking down at her, he was struck by how beautiful she was. Her golden hair fanned out on the tan duvet, her brown eyes vibrant, her cheeks and chest flushed.

"Damn, you're beautiful," he stated.

"Paddy," she looked up at him. "Shut up. It's been too long. I know we don't have a lot of time so you're going to have to make it quick." That sobered him up. Those words were the same she used fifteen months ago just before they broke up.

When she reached for his belt, he stayed her hands. "No," he said. She looked up at him confused. Cupping her jaw, he stoked her cheek. "No, love, when I make love to you, *tonight,* I want it to be perfect. And I want to take my time. I don't want *quick* with you. You don't deserve it and I will always give you what you deserve."

Their gazes stayed locked for a long moment but soon Keera nodded, and Paddy let out a breath.

"Sorry I sort of... jumped you. I really really want you."

"Hey, never apologize," he winked as he moved to the side of the bed. "I really want you too, you have no idea. But, love, I don't want to rush, and we should get ready. We only have an hour."

"Should we hurry? What's the line going to be like?" she scurried off the bed.

"No worries, I have VIP access," he replied. "Besides, they won't start without me."

She stopped at the door of the bathroom. "Paddy," she began. "TS Jameson..."

"What about him?"

"Tell me the truth... it's not *you*, is it? I mean, I've seen the profile pictures on the backs of the books but..."

He grinned. "No," he shook his head. "I'm not that old."

"But you know him... well?"

"I do," he replied. "But that's all the answers you're going to get."

She pursed her lips together, looking as adorable as he had ever seen.

"Fine, but I expect answers later."

He said nothing, as she closed the bathroom door. Chuckling, he went over to his small weekend suitcase and sent a text to his uncle.

Paddy: Made it to the hotel.

Uncle Tully: Should I have them hold for an hour or did she shut you down?

Paddy: Haha, my idea not to, actually.

Uncle Tully: What the hell's wrong with you, lad?

Paddy: I didn't want to rush. We'll be there on time. Promise. The longer we wait the more receptive she'll be, I promise you that.

Uncle Tully: Fair enough. See you soon.

Paddy set the phone on the bed. Pulling out his black suit pants and blazer, he dressed quickly putting an order in with room service for a bottle of champagne to be brought up.

He was fixing his cuffs when there was a knock on the door. Pulling it open, he thanked the waiter, tipped him and closed the door. Keera was still in the bathroom, but Paddy popped the cork and poured. As expected, Keera opened the door to see what the noise was. When he turned, his breath caught. She had curled her hair and darkened her eyes; he was fairly certain it was called smoky eye but did not care at that moment. She looked stunning. She stepped out of the bathroom wearing a thigh high black silk slip, dark pantyhose, and no shoes.

"Ooh, how did you know?" she questioned, stepping fully out of the bathroom to him.

Shaking himself out of the stupor, he handed her a glass and kept the other. Clinking his glass to hers, they sipped, and he eyed her over the rim of the flute.

"Should I be jealous?" he asked.

"Of what?"

"Of TS? You're dressing up this much for him..."

She stepped up to him and spoke, her voice low, sultry. "Who says I'm dressing up for him?"

Paddy swallowed the champagne and grinned.

"Now, since you purchased this amazing bottle, how about you let me pull on my dress and we can enjoy the drink as we look out on the River Shannon?"

"Sounds good," Paddy answered, topping her glass off. She rose on her tippy-toes and placed a gentle kiss on his lips.

"Thank you for all of this, Paddy."

"I love you," Paddy said and reveled in her grin. Again, a short, all-too-quick kiss on his lips and she hurried back to the bathroom. Paddy watched her go, then moved to the window and gazed out.

It didn't take long for the bathroom door to open again, and Keera stepped out. Paddy turned and his jaw dropped. The black dress fell to her mid-thigh, the tight material hugged every inch of her body. The high heels she wore would have brought him to his knees had he not wanted to feel her against him. A quick breath out and then he moved faster than she expected. Grabbing her, he pulled her flush against him and took in her gorgeous face.

"Damn, you're beautiful," he sighed and captured her lips with his.

The feeling of her giving in and sagging against him all while kissing him back was a feeling he wanted to bottle up. She was not tentative in her movements as she had been the first time they kissed. She was far more experienced, and a part of Paddy swelled with pride to have been the first to teach her, but another part hesitated. He hated the fact she had been with other men, but he suppressed it. He had no room to judge or talk. Still, when she slid her tongue to fight alongside his, he couldn't help his thoughts. How many others had felt that same thing? And like a bucket of cold water poured over him, he pulled back and gently stroked her arm.

"What's wrong?" she asked. "You tensed up on me."

"I'm sorry," he admitted.

"Talk to me?" she pleaded.

"Don't be angry," he begged.

"I won't."

"How many guys were you with in America?" he winced as he said it, waiting for her wrath. He had no right, but he needed to know.

Surprisingly, she sighed and sat on the bed, her arms wrapped around herself. "That really bothers you, huh?"

"It shouldn't, I know, and I love you no matter what. I'm hardly one to say anything... I just need to know."

She nodded slowly. "You told me about Stephanie. Okay, I'll tell you. Three," she looked up at him. "I've been with three men other than you. Dylan and Max in American and Patrick here in Ireland. And honestly Max and I were pretty serious. Up until my final month, we were talking about him moving to Ireland, but I realized it wouldn't ever work, and... god, this is going to sound so stalkerish... I looked you up on social media a few times and even tried to get information from Emmet when he called. I realized how much I missed you and how I measured every guy to you. Though Dylan and Max were cute, fun even, they lacked a very large part... they weren't you." She looked up at him. "I talk a big game as they say in America, but honestly, I... I only want you."

His heart lightened and he knelt before her. Taking her hands in his, he smiled when she looked at him.

"I love you, Keera. Thank you for sharing that with me. I'm sorry for being such a..."

"Neanderthal?" she provided.

He chuckled. "Aye, that's a good term." Leaning forward, he placed a gentle kiss on her lips and laughed when she smacked his arm.

"You are such a caveman."

"Yes, but you love me, don't forget," he winked just as his phone rang an alarm. Standing, he snatched it off the table near the bottle of champagne.

"It's a pity we only get four glasses out of this," she said lifting the bottle out of the ice bucket and topping off their glasses, successfully finishing the bottle.

Paddy pocketed his phone, took his glass and clinked it with hers.

"To me being your first choice and the best you ever had."

"I'm not drinking to that," she teased. "*Besides* stroking your ego, I said nothing about you being the best."

"You can't deny it," he winked.

She huffed but didn't back down. "To us," she proposed. "Years together, years apart, but it's the years to come that hold my heart."

Paddy cocked his head to one side. "Beautiful, O'Quinn."

"Poetry isn't usually my thing but hey, the moment called for it." Paddy took a drink, never dropping her gaze. His phone rang again. "Does that mean we have to go?" she asked. He nodded. "Why am I nervous?"

"Don't be. He's going to love you."

"I hope so," she sighed.

"Come on, let's get going. I can't wait to introduce you two."

Taking her head, he pocketed his phone, turned on a light by the bed, and made sure he had his room key. Then, he led her down the hall and out to the streets of Limerick toward the museum where TS Jameson waited.

Chapter

Seventeen

Paddy led the way down the street to the city museum. Sliding between the large pillars in the front of the weathered brick building, Keera watched as Paddy pulled out two tickets and handed them to the young woman at the door. She looked at them and smiled.

"Welcome, Mr. O'Shea," she said. "And Miss…"

"O'Quinn," Keera provided.

"Miss O'Quinn," she smiled. "Please follow me. You are in our VIP lounge. Mr. Jameson is ready to start as soon as you arrived. I'll let him know."

They followed the young brunette down a hallway and up some stairs as she spoke. "Included in the VIP ticket are complimentary drinks from the bar, some light hors d'oeuvres, and a meet and greet with Mr. Jameson." She opened the doors to a room, overlooking a small stage. Several other people were in the room, milling about, only looking up when they walked in. Below them, nearer the stage were about one hundred people seated in the auditorium.

"We will be lifting the privacy screens shortly. Can I get you anything to drink?" the woman asked, making her way to the bar in the corner.

"A whiskey for me," Paddy said. "The reserve, please," he pointed to the bottle. "Kee?"

"I'll stick with champagne," she replied.

The woman smiled and began making the drinks. Paddy stood beside her, a sort of nervous energy radiating off him. When they took their drinks, he turned to her and clinked his glass to hers.

The woman stepped out from behind the bar and onto a small stage by the privacy screen covered window.

"Ladies and gentlemen, welcome. My name is Stacy and I will be your personal VIP companion tonight. If you would like another drink before TS Jameson begins, please come over to the bar now. If you see any hors d'oeuvres running low, please do not hesitate to let me know. Anything I can do to make your time with us special, just let me know. I will radio down to the stage director to let her know we are ready, and I'll be right there to refill drinks."

A couple people lined up at the bar and it gave Paddy and Keera a chance to take it all in. They moved to the window and looked out at the crowd below.

"This is such an interesting venue," Keera said.

"Yeah, he always picks the one place that means something to his book," Paddy explained. "He held this at the university when it was a story about a group of students getting into trouble and there was a professor detective. And he picked the culinary school down the road when his book, *Flay-Mignon* was released."

"And for *The President's Secret?*"

"People's Park."

"Brilliant," she replied. "So, this next book has to do with a museum?"

"A curator detective."

"Fascinating," she replied. "I am so very excited to meet him."

"Not long now," Paddy stated still looking down at the stage.

Turning to him, she slid her arm through his and rested her head on his arm.

"Thank you, Paddy," she said. "I can't tell you how happy this makes me."

His soft hum lightened her heart. "Me too, love."

"Ladies and gentlemen, welcome to Limerick City Museum," a disembodied voice came over the loudspeaker. The one-way windows opened, and the VIP guests gathered around. "As a reminder, in the case of an emergency, walk calmly to the exits. Flash photography and recording devices are strictly prohibited. And now, it is our privilege to introduce, finishing his international book tour; Limerick's very own, Mr. TS Jameson."

Applause echoed throughout the auditorium as the curtain parted and a man stepped out, dressed in a suit with the collar of his button up shirt unbuttoned, his shoulder length, dark grey hair, and light grey beard shimmering in the stage lights. He smiled and his eyes trailed up to the VIP booth. Locking eyes with Paddy, he raised an eyebrow and smirked. Keera knew that smirk anywhere.

Paddy clapped and cheered beside her, but his grin was a mile wide. Not only had she seen that man before, she saw the eerie echo of Paddy in his face.

"Thank you, thank you," TS Jameson said. "Well, well, that's a better greeting than I got in London, so it is."

The voice matched her memory, too. "TS..." Keera breathed, then sighed. "Uncle Tully."

Paddy turned to her. "Surprise," he whispered.

"Oh, you are in so much trouble," she replied but couldn't help her smile.

He wrapped his arm around her waist and moved his lips close to her ear.

"I look forward to it," his hot breath and implied connotation caused a shiver to race up her spine. When he pulled back, she leaned in to kiss him, but paused.

"You have no idea how bad you're going to get it, mister."

She felt his lips widen in a grin that quickly turned to a soft groan. "Hurry up, Uncle Tully," he whispered.

She giggled. "Pay back for this afternoon. We have his talk here, the meet and greet, and then dinner. You have brought this on yourself."

"Anticipation is key here, love," he stated. "Are *you* sure you want to play this game?" his bouncing eyebrows made her laugh. She promptly covered her mouth with her hand when someone shushed her.

With a final look at Paddy, she turned back to the window and looked out to see TS Jameson, also known as Uncle Tully, speaking to the audience about his journey as a writer. Paddy's hand rested on her lower back just above the curve of her hips. His thumb rubbing innocent circles. She squirmed under his touch but kept her eyes on her favorite author speaking below.

The second Paddy's Uncle Tully walked out on stage, Paddy felt Keera's surprise. He was buzzing as soon as they left the hotel together. The whiskey had helped but as soon as his uncle stepped out on stage, he let out an exhale of relief. She wasn't angry with him, instead she was teasing him.

He could not wait to introduce her to TS Jameson. Once the speech was over, Uncle Tully took questions from the auditorium audience and soon bade them goodbye, left the stage, and made his way up to the VIP lounge.

Stacy, the VIP Concierge, stepped over to the back door and called out. "If I could have everyone's attention. It is my privilege to introduce one of my favorite authors, TS Jameson."

The door opened and Tully walked in as applause erupted. Once the crowd quieted down, he smiled at her. "Flattery will get you everywhere, my dear... but *one of* not your *absolute* favorite? I'm disappointed."

Stacy giggled. "Oh, Mr. Jameson, I didn't want to sound too much of a sycophant."

"You don't want it to go to my head, more like," he grinned.

"Too late for that!" Paddy called out jovially. Tully's eyes scanned the room, landing on Paddy, his arm around Keera's shoulders.

"You should know, same blood and all that," Tully teased back. "Ladies and gentlemen," he motioned to Paddy. "My nephew."

The VIPs nodded and murmurs of delight and affirmation twittered around the small room.

"Mr. Jameson, please come this way." Stacy motioned toward the platform she had stood on earlier. "Can I get you something to drink?"

"A whiskey, my dear, the reserve, please," he said. Paddy raised his glass toward him indicating he made a good choice.

"Uncle Tully always requests they have a bottle or two available at his events," Paddy explained. "It's his favorite."

Keera wasn't listening, she was clearly mesmerized.

Once Tully had his drink in hand, everyone was requested to have a seat in the cozy setting. Paddy and Keera sat to Tully's left. Throughout the next forty minutes, Tully answered questions from the much smaller audience, then he sat at the small table beside the stage where copies of his book, *Missing from the Collection* lay.

"At this time, ladies and gentlemen, Mr. Jameson will be signing advanced copies of his latest book. The books are complimentary with your VIP ticket! Please line up to claim your copy. Afterwards, you are welcome to stay and have another drink or two. I will begin to shut the bar down in an hour. Again, please don't hesitate to ask for my assistance with any of your needs."

The group moved together, and Paddy felt the excitement from Keera next to him. "Now you don't have to wait for me to finish my copy," he teased.

"Thank god, you are the slowest reader I know," she giggled as they took their place in line.

Chapter Eighteen

I can't believe it! Keera wanted to shout for joy. Not only was she meeting Paddy's uncle, but that uncle was TS Jameson. She didn't ask any questions during the Q&A but really wanted to pick his brain about getting published. She may have lied a little when she told Paddy she only had scribblings. She actually had a full manuscript and the four people she let read it, loved it. But then again, they were her family, so they were all forced to like it. She would love to get a true mystery writer's opinion. Though she was pretty sure he'd say it was shite.

Please don't let me make a fool of myself, she thought as they took the last step to Tully's table.

"Paddy!" Tully smiled and stood, giving him a back-slapping hug. "I've missed you. It's good to see you."

"And you, Uncle," Paddy said. Then, pulling back, he looked over at Keera. "This is Keera."

"My goodness, love. He definitely did well for himself," Tully teased.

"She's a big fan and I promised to introduce you."

"Oh hush, Paddy," Tully said with a wink and looked expectantly at Keera.

"It's so wonderful to meet you!" Keera couldn't hold back. "I have read everything you have ever written."

"Oh, dear, I hope you didn't find a copy of my university thesis," he teased. "It's dull stuff."

"No, no, everything published, I guess. Not that your thesis wasn't published, I mean... ehm..." she stopped and thought a second. Tully's amused gaze on her. "I want to be a writer too. Oh, my god, I'm sorry, that must be so annoying. You probably get at least three people telling you that every day."

"Sometimes five," he teased. "But none as pretty as you. And most of the time my favorite is; *you should write my life story. It would be a bestseller!*" Tully chuckled.

Keera giggled. "Well, my life is definitely crazy but it's no mystery. I love how you weave a story! It keeps me guessing until the very end."

"What sort of stories to you write?" Tully asked.

"Mystery," she replied. "But nothing as great as you."

"Don't sell yourself short," Tully stated. "I'd love to take a look."

"Really? That would be amazing." Someone cleared their throat behind them.

"Let me get these signed and I'll meet you two for dinner." He looked over at Paddy. "You have the name of the restaurant?" Paddy nodded. "Good." Tully sat back down and grabbed one of the books. Signing a message to her, he closed the book and handed it to her.

Keera took it like it was the most precious gift in the world. "Thank you," she breathed.

"You are very welcome, and I look forward to having dinner together tonight. Maybe we can wear this one out and it'll just be you and me. I can share some embarrassing baby stories."

"I'd love that," she laughed.

"Uncle Tully," Paddy complained.

"He was a cute kid... not sure what happened," Tully winked. "Now," he leaned back. "I'm going to hold on to your copy, Paddy since you already have one." His eyes drifted to Stacy who was refilling a wine glass and wiping down the bar for the final time.

"Good idea," Paddy agreed. "Don't make her fall in love with you though."

Tully nearly choked on his whiskey. "She's like... twelve," he replied.

"Not even close. See you soon," Paddy answered placing a hand on Keera's back.

Tully shook his head as he watched them leave. Keera was sure she heard him mumble something that sounded like *damn, kid.* Then laugh.

Paddy and Keera stepped over to the side, nearest the door. Keera opened the front cover of her book to read what he wrote.

Keera–

He's always loved you, you know. I can understand why. Please don't hurt him.

Keep writing and follow your dreams.

TS Jameson

Keera bit her lip as tears pricked the back of her eyes.

"What did he write?" Paddy asked, looking over her

shoulder.

Keera promptly closed the hardback cover. "Nothing."

"Oh, no fair," he replied. "You read mine."

"You handed it to me," she reminded him. "And don't even try to sneak up and steal it."

Paddy took a step back and looked her up and down. "Tempting."

"Good," she bit her lip.

Paddy let out a breath and downed his whiskey. "Damn." He didn't look at her.

Keera had to stop herself from doing cheers. He was just as affected as she was. They both still wanted each other. She was looking forward to dinner with Tully, but she was also very much looking forward to that evening back at the hotel with Paddy.

They waited at a four-top table, at a beautiful restaurant for Tully to join them. Paddy held her hand as they spoke low. He wanted to know what his uncle had written in the book but decided on not asking again, for now. Instead, he turned the conversation to her family, steering well clear of Emmet's woes so as to not bring her down from the high she was riding. They were so intently focused on each other, they did not see Uncle Tully walk up until he cleared his throat. Looking over at him, he raised an eyebrow.

"Maybe it is a good thing you got a hotel room, lad," he teased. It's not like you would pay any attention to me anyway."

"Sorry, Uncle Tully," Paddy grinned. "But when I have this beautiful woman before me, I don't pay attention to anything else."

Uncle Tully nodded slowly and then pulled out the notebook he always carried with him. Jotting a note down, he looked up at Keera's questioning gaze.

"Some youngsters have their phones to take notes, but I like good old-fashioned pen and paper. Loverboy just gave me an idea for a new story."

"At least, I'm good for something," Paddy chuckled and offered the chair opposite him.

"Awe, you're good for many things, love," Keera replied.

"Whatever you say, darlin'."

"Well, at least you're starting on the right foot," Tully winked as he placed the napkin on his lap. "Two most important words to learn early are, *yes, dear.*"

Paddy laughed outright. "Forgive me, Uncle, but I don't think I should take relationship advice from a confirmed bachelor."

Tully acquiesced jovially as the waitress came around to take their order.

Chapter

Nineteen

After Tully ordered a glass of whiskey, Paddy topped off Keera's wine glass. Once the bruschetta appetizer was placed before them along with Tully's whiskey, Tully raised the glass and made a toast.

"To family and friends. You can't choose your family, but I've been damn lucky." He tilted the drink toward Paddy. "You can choose friends and we're lucky when they become like family." He looked over at Keera. "I'm proud to say I know you both."

"To your great success, Uncle Tully. And with thanks for all you've done for me. I love you," Paddy said.

"Don't lose your balls on me now," Tully said but Keera could see that even though he was teasing, his smile was genuine.

They drank and dug into the starter.

"So, tell me, lass," Tully looked at her as he wiped his mouth with the ivory colored, cloth napkin. "What got you into writing?"

She took a bite and groaned silently. Her immediate answer would only cause him to laugh. But knowing Tully, he would wave it off.

"You did," she finally answered.

"I'm flattered," as expected he continued, "but what really got you into writing?"

She thought a moment. "Honestly, it was when I was in school. My teachers were all amazing except one; Ms. Gunther. She was perhaps the dullest teacher I've ever had. One day, I forgot the book I was reading. I would usually read in the back to alleviate boredom. It was actually your *Coffee Bean Murders* and I pulled out my notebook trying to think where you were going with the plot. I tried to think like you and began writing scenarios."

"Were you right?" he asked.

Keera nodded after taking a sip of her wine. "One of my lesser theories actually. I didn't think you would make it the loving son."

"Exactly," Tully said. "So that's what made you want to write? Trying not to be bored in class?"

"Heh, yeah," Keera breathed a laugh.

"Do you have a manuscript written?"

She looked sheepishly at Paddy. "Yeah."

"Wait, you told me you only have jottings," Paddy said.

"I know," she replied. "It's only... I've only let my ma, aunt, uncle and Emmet read my work. I didn't want you to hate it."

"I could never hate it," Paddy answered taking her hand.

"But that's the other thing... Everyone says it's amazing and they loved it but, what if they're just trying to be nice? What if it really sucks and nobody wants to read it?"

"Congratulations," Uncle Tully leaned back. "You have officially become an author." Keera looked at him, confused. "Darlin', I've been at this for..." he thought a moment. "Dear god, forty years. And I still, to this day have that fear. Trust me, the manuscript I'm working on right now has me panicked but the best thing to do, is to let someone you trust read it. Are you proud of it?" he asked.

Keera thought a moment. "Yes, but..."

Uncle Tully held up his hand. "No, that's all you need to know. If you're proud of your work, you know what I tell anyone who doesn't like it? Sod off."

Keera giggled, a load of worry lifting from her shoulders. The waiter came around with their food and refilled their water glasses.

"Would you permit me to read it?" Tully asked after they ate for a minute.

Keera took a deep breath. "Yeah, I would like that."

"And what about me?" Paddy questioned.

"Maybe," she teased.

"Love you too," Paddy rolled his eyes.

"You know you'll lose out to age and experience every time, Paddy," Uncle Tully said.

"Speaking of your age," Paddy started.

"Didn't think we were but, okay."

"How did you leave it with Stacy? Did she enjoy the book?" Paddy wiggled his brows.

"Ecstatic, but I told her not to fall in love with me."

"I bet you did, too, you old goat."

"Let's get one thing clear…" Tully began. "I am *not* old. A lot of good years left in me with the right woman." He winked at Keera.

She laughed outright. "Sorry, I was just thinking about how much my mother would pounce on you."

"In a good way?" his eyes twinkled making Keera laugh even more.

"Very possibly."

"That's all I'd need," Paddy stated drinking his wine. "God help me."

"Aren't you supposed to be helping your old uncle?"

"Helping him by getting him with my girlfriend's mother?"

"Why not? If she's as pretty as this one, I'd be very fortunate," Tully replied.

The rest of their evening passed in much the same fashion. Keera enjoyed watching Tully and Paddy interact. They laughed together when Tully told a story about a five-year-old Paddy when. But they all steered clear of the burning topic. What happened to Paddy's parents? Keera knew they died when Paddy was ten, but she didn't know how. Instead of bringing the group down, she said nothing, even though she burned to know.

Finally, it was time to leave and as Tully snatched the check before Paddy could, he pulled out some euros and paid.

Stepping out of the restaurant, they heard music playing from somewhere nearby. Uncle Tully took a deep breath in and hummed. He clenched and unclenched his fist before he stuffed his hands in his pockets.

"There's nothing like a beautiful clear evening on the water," he said.

"Could we walk a bit?" Keera asked. "It's so beautiful out."

"You kids go ahead," Tully replied. "I know what it's like to be young. I'm heading home. I'm tired today, all the travelling has caught up with me."

"We'll see you tomorrow?" Paddy embraced his uncle.

"Absolutely," Tully agreed. "How long are you staying?"

"No definite plans. We're staying two nights at the Pier. Figured you could put us up if we want to stay longer."

"Of course," Tully nodded. "You're always welcome." He smiled then grunted and rolled his shoulder.

"You okay?" Paddy asked concerned.

"Yeah, yeah, just a tight muscle spasm. I'm fine, lad. You enjoy your night," he winked, cupped his face and smiled. Then, turning to Keera, he embraced her. "Keep my boy in line," he chuckled. "I'm so happy to have met you."

"Me too, and I will," she answered.

"I'm looking forward to reading your book."

She instantly grew nervous but nodded.

"See you later," he tossed over his shoulder as he headed for the taxi line.

Paddy looked back at Keera. "Wanna walk?"

"Oh yes," she answered. "It's such a beautiful evening. But not too long. I want you, O'Shea."

He took her hand, raised it to his lips and kissed her knuckles all while keeping his eyes locked with hers. "I know we've already said this, but I need to tell you; I love you, Keera. I've never said it to anyone else. Only you. And I know now, I'll never say it to anyone other than you."

She stepped closer to him and wrapped her arms around him.

"I love you too, Paddy. I've never said it to anyone else either. Only you and I will never grow tired of hearing you say it."

He cupped her face and pulled her close, kissing her gently, languidly, lovingly. As soon as he pulled back, her soft eyes and gentle smile spoke volumes.

"On second thought... the walk can wait," Keera said. "Take me back to the hotel, Paddy. I want you."

He could record those words and never tire of hearing them either.

Chapter Twenty

Keera reached beside her as the early morning sun streamed through the curtains. Her hand met cool sheets but no Paddy. Sitting up, she looked around the room. It was empty.

"Paddy?" she called out, hoping he was in the restroom or out in the main sitting area.

No answer.

Swallowing hard, she pulled the sheet around her, clasping it around her chest, under her arms. Padding to the sitting room, she looked around. He wasn't there.

Icy dread seeped its way into her mind. She tried to shake it off, but it was there to stay. Their first time together was eerily similar to what was happening. She remembered waking up with a smile that quickly turned to confusion as she saw him sitting on the bed fully dressed pulling on his shoes.

She remembered asking him what he was doing, and she remembered his words all too well.

"You're cute but young, Keera. I prefer my women a little more... experienced. We can be friends though, right?"

She was shocked and hurt. She remembered how he leaned over the bed, kissed her forehead, grabbed his jacket, and left the room. He hadn't come back, nor texted her for a week. When he did, she went right back to him. And she did it again over and over.

Nothing had changed. After everything they went through, after the night before... he hadn't changed. Cursing the feeling of tears on her cheeks, she went back to the bedroom and grabbed a pair of jeans, a t-shirt, and her shoes. She cursed the tears again as her vision blurred when she tried to get her shoes on.

The tell-tale click of the lock made her pause. The door opened and Paddy walked in with a drink carrier and a bag of something that smelled of cinnamon, icing, and dough.

Keera looked out of the bedroom when he set the food down on the small table.

"Hey honey, I'm home," he grinned then his smile fell, and his brows furrowed. "Keera? What's wrong? What happened?" He rushed to her pulling her to him. She didn't hug him back.

"Where were you?" she questioned pushing away.

"I went to get coffee and breakfast. Baby, what's wrong? What happened? Why are you crying?"

"Why did you leave me?"

"Leave you? What?" he pulled back. "Baby, I wanted to get coffee. Are you okay?"

"No, I'm not. You left and it made me... remember."

"Remember what?" he asked confused.

"When you left me that morning after our first time."

He froze. "Oh, love, I'm so sorry. I wanted to get you breakfast in bed. But the line was longer than I anticipated. I'm so sorry about our first time, too. Keera, I..." he huffed a sigh. "I can't go back and change how much of a bastard I was to you but I can tell you... the reason I left the way I did that morning was because I told you I loved you." She looked at him and he sat down on the foot of the bed. "When you fell asleep, I... I whispered I loved you and it freaked me out. I had never said that before to anyone. I acted like a jerk because I thought maybe that would make you see I wasn't a good guy and you'd leave me just like every other relationship I've had. But you didn't. I love you, Keera. I've always loved you and I am so happy you gave me another shot and another and another, over and over again when I messed up. I'm so sorry I left you then and I'm sorry my leaving this morning caused you to remember. But the truth is, I want forever with you. I want a family. I want to wake up and get you coffee and breakfast every day for the rest of my life. I see my future with you and you alone. I want you to succeed in your dream of being a writer. I want to help you in every way I can. Support you however I can. I want to marry you. I want to go back to that incompetent doctor and hear him say you *are* pregnant with *my* child. I want it all."

Keera stared at him for a long time. So many emotions, words, and truths were rushing through her. Just as she was about to reply, frantic knocking echoed in the room.

Dammit, of all times... of all the times to be interrupted, it had to be then, because, of course it did.

The knocking didn't stop and became more and more insistent. With an expletive, he stalked to the door and ripped it open. He came face to face with a man he had never seen before, dressed in a suit holding a key.

"What?" Paddy spat.

"Paddy," his eyes were drawn to the man standing beside the one in a suit.

"Markus?" Paddy questioned. "What the hell are you doing here?"

"It's your uncle, Paddy," Markus, Tully's agent started. Paddy felt all blood drain from his face, and he weaved for a moment.

"Uncle Tully? What happened?"

"He had a heart attack on the way home last night," Markus stated.

"Oh, my god, is he okay?" Keera raced to the door. Paddy was grateful she asked. He couldn't bring himself to say anything. His mouth was dry.

"He's in the hospital," was the answer.

"Is he… is he alive?" Paddy finally asked.

"Yes."

"Oh, thank god," Keera leaned against him. "Can we see him?"

"That's why I'm here. Get a coat it's about to rain."

Sure enough, as if his emotions could control the weather, Paddy looked out the window. Where once was bright morning sunlight, now was dark dreary clouds.

The drive to the hospital was the longest of Paddy's entire life. His uncle was alive, that's all he had to remember. But he couldn't shake the feeling his life was collapsing around him. Keera sat beside him in the backseat, his hand in hers, her thumb rubbing across his knuckles. He looked down at their hands, then up into her eyes.

"He'll be okay," she said.

"I can't lose him," his voice cracked. "He's all I have."

She squeezed his hand. "You have me, too," she declared. "I'm not going anywhere and... about what you said earlier? I want it too, with you. Let's talk more later, okay?"

Taking a deep breath, he sighed in relief. They pulled up to the hospital and Markus looked back at them. "He's been checked in but I'm not sure what room. I'll park and follow. You go."

"Thank you," Paddy said and threw open the door. Not thinking about helping Keera out, he was halfway to the door when he remembered. Thankfully, she was right behind him. The hospital door opened and the usual blast of recycled air along with the pungent smell of disinfectant, hit them both. It churned his stomach, but he hurried to the receptionist and was thankful when she looked up immediately.

"Good morning," she said pleasantly.

"Ehm, hi, my uncle was admitted last night, and I was wanting to see him, please."

"Of course, what is his name?" she turned to the computer.

"Tulliver Sebastian Jameson," she said.

Keera giggled beside him. Glancing over, he saw a twinkle in her eyes.

"Tulliver?" she questioned.

Paddy shrugged as a near hysterical chuckle escaped his lips.

"Please wear these visitor badges and follow me," the receptionist smiled handing two clip on badges and waved them through. Paddy and Keera passed through the security door she had buzzed open. Following her down the short hallway, they came to a set of elevators.

"Mr. Jameson is in room 321. Third floor, turn left when the elevator doors open," she explained.

"Thank you so much," Paddy said and stepped into the elevator.

"When you leave, just leave the badges at the front desk." She instructed just as the doors closed.

Once they reached the third floor, they turned left, and Paddy's shaking hands began to sweat.

"What do you mean I can't have coffee?"

His heart lifted considerably when he heard his uncle's voice.

"Sir, you just had a heart attack. You are not allowed coffee."

"Listen here, I never have missed a day of coffee in my life. Now get me someone I can talk to. I can't work without coffee."

"Sir, you need to be resting."

"Damn it all to hell, I'm not resting! I have a deadline!"

Paddy walked to the door of 321 and looked in. His uncle was sitting up in the hospital bed, wearing one of the fashionless hospital gowns. His shoulder length hair was pulled up, away from his face and neck and machine hook ups were attached to various parts of his body. Pages of his manuscript were in his hand. The nurse attending him was standing beside the currently beeping machine with a look of exasperation on her face.

"Already making friends, Uncle Tully?" Paddy asked.

Tully's eyes snapped to the door. "I told Markus not to worry you. I'm fine."

Paddy walked in. Keera close behind. "What happened?" Paddy walked over to the other side of the bed and sat in one of the chairs.

"I decided to walk home last night instead of taking a taxi... you know, *exercise*," he enunciated the last word angling toward the nurse, who didn't react.

"That's over a ten-minute drive, let alone walking! What were you thinking?" Paddy demanded.

"I was thinking I am a grown man and can make my own choices without my *nephew* disrespecting me."

Paddy huffed a sigh. "I'm sorry. But look what happened!"

"What happened is neither here nor there. They said I had a New Stem, whatever the hell that is and elevated trampolines."

"NSTEMI and elevated *troponin*," the nurse corrected.

"Yeah, that," Tully replied.

"What does that mean?" Paddy asked.

"It means the affected artery was only partially blocked. Troponin is an enzyme. It's naturally in your body but when it is elevated that means the heart has secreted it when cardiac cells die. He's scheduled to have a stent put in later today but until then, he's NPO."

"NPO?" Paddy questioned.

"*Nil per os,* nothing by mouth," the nurse clarified as she moved toward the door with his chart.

"Damn Nazis. I'll have you know, my father fought against this sort of injustice!" He called after the nurse as she left the room.

"Come on, Uncle Tully, she's only doing her job."

"I'm on deadline, lad. How the hell am I supposed to focus without coffee? Let alone the hours spent here. They tell me after the stents are put in, I'll have a recovery period. Do you know what that means? I'll be too far behind my schedule. Markus cancelled my Dublin signing next week as it is. It was supposed to be an encore talk. People are expecting me! My fans are expecting me! I can't let them down."

"Yes, you can," Markus' voice came from the door. "You need to rest."

"You tell that to Declan. He clearly has no idea. Already had three texts from him today."

"Declan is Uncle Tully's editor," Paddy whispered to Keera as Tully and Markus continued.

"Did you read said texts?" Markus asked Tully.

"Don't need to," Tully muttered. "*Where's the manuscript? Where are the pages you promised me? Don't make me have to extend the deadline* again *just because you're in the hospital.*"

Markus huffed, stalked over to the other side of the bed and grabbed the phone from the tray. Pulling up the texts, he read. "*You better still be alive, you bastard. I'll kill you myself if you aren't.* Next one; *take good care of yourself. For all our sakes. Be careful, friend.* Last one; *Don't worry about the pages owed. I've talked to Doug and he said the same as we all do; take it easy, get better. We all love you, you old goat.*"

Tully grumbled. "He goes from calling me a bastard to a friend to saying he loves me then calls me old."

"Rest up, keep me posted on your health. I'm going to call him now. Doug needs to know, too," Markus said walking out of the room, clicking on his phone.

Tully looked over at Keera. "You sure you want in on this circus? I have my agent, my editor, and now the owner of the publishing company contacting me." He rolled his eyes, adjusted in the bed, and flinched. Paddy jumped up to help. Once he was situated, Tully looked up at Paddy to see the tears glistening in his light brown eyes.

"Hey, lad, I'm all right," he said. Paddy nodded quickly but wouldn't look him in the eyes.

"Hey," Tully grasped the back of Paddy's neck and pulled him down. Pressing his forehead to his nephew's, Tully forced him to look at him. "I'm not going anywhere for a long time, aye? Besides, I promised you I'd be the cool great-uncle and you haven't given me any grandnephews or nieces yet."

He grinned then when Paddy nodded and let out a breath, Tully broke away and kissed his forehead. Paddy took a step back when the nurse came in again this time with some pills. Wiping his eyes, Paddy walked over to Keera. Her stomach growled.

"I'm going to get us something from the canteen. We haven't had anything for breakfast," Paddy stated.

"See if you can sneak up a cup of coffee," Tully called after him. Paddy just shook his head.

Keera took his hand as they walked together. They said nothing until they were nearer to the cafeteria.

"You really love him," she said.

"He took me in when my parents died."

"You never said how they died."

Paddy didn't say anything. They ordered their breakfast and as they waited for the food, Paddy put his hands in his pockets and spoke low.

"Ma and Da' were doctors. They had me pretty late, Ma was thirty-five. They were part of the *Doctors Without Borders* program. They were on a six-month tour. I was staying with my grandparents. There was a bombing near their camp. I was told they were part of five doctors who ran to help those injured but as soon as they were there, another bomb exploded, and everyone was killed. Including my parents."

Keera took his hand but said nothing. "My other aunts and uncles wanted nothing to do with me. Bad blood, I guess. My grandparents were told several times to put me up for adoption. They were getting older and couldn't keep up with me. My Uncle Tully was just back from his book tour and his latest had been a number one bestseller for three consecutive quarters. There was also talk of a movie deal. But he heard what my father's brother said about me... about giving me up, how I wasn't their problem. Tully lost it on them. Told them all how disgusting and despicable they were. And how he was glad his sister was dead so she didn't have to hear how they were speaking about her son. I was listening at the top of the stairs and soon he marched up, told me to pack my bags. I was going to be staying with him. He sacrificed his movie deal for me. They needed him in LA at the end of the month and he refused. Knowing I needed consistency and staying home in Limerick was part of that. I needed to settle in with him and mourn my parents. He bought hurling gear instead of a new sports car. He bought school uniforms instead of a plane ticket to anywhere he could have wanted. He went to parent-teacher meetings instead of going out on a date. He sacrificed so much for me. I'll never be able to pay him back. So yeah, I really love him. He's the only father I truly know." His voice quivered. "I can't lose him."

"Hey," Keera moved to stand in front of him. "You won't. He's okay. The doctors are confident. He'll be fine."

Paddy nodded quickly and looked away from her. "Are *we* okay?"

Keera took a deep breath and squeezed his hands. "I'll not lie, you dumping all of your feelings on me was... not expected and a bit... scary. But I want it all too. I want to be with you. I just don't really want kids right now I never thought I would want them until the scare. But I wasn't against marrying *you,* I was just against marriage. I guess I saw a lot with my cousins and the hell Sean went through when Innis and Trish slept together and the only healthy marriage I had to base anything on was Uncle Orin and Aunt Dee and Cabhan and Rachael. But that was only two and the others... I didn't want the worry or pain. But only after you poured your heart out did I realize, what I was losing by saying no." Paddy's eyes grew wide. Keera kissed his hand. "I want this... you."

A relieved grin spread across his face and he gently cupped her face.

"I love you, Keera O'Quinn. Always have. Always will."

She sighed happily and kissed him. Only when they heard someone clear their throats and call Paddy's name, did they turn to the counter and take the food they had ordered.

After they ate in silence for a little while, Paddy wiped his mouth with a paper napkin and leaned back.

"Let's go back upstairs," he said. "Check in with Uncle Tully and see what the doctors say."

Keera agreed and they headed back up, but Paddy couldn't stop the shaking in his fingers. It scared him, but as soon as Keera squeezed his hand, he let out a breath. She was still there. He could get through anything with her by his side.

Chapter Twenty-One

As soon as they reached Tully's room, Paddy saw the doctors speaking to him. Keera hung back and let go of his hand. Turning to her, he searched her gaze.

"Go. I'm going to check in with ma and see how Emmet is doing."

He nodded then knocked on the door to announce himself. The two people in white coats turned.

"Paddy, my lad, come in. This is my nephew," Tully said. "Butcher One and Two are just going over what to expect."

Paddy shook hands with both doctors.

"We were just telling your uncle, he's scheduled to receive the stent at three. There will be two placed in the left anterior descending and the circumflex artery. Both were impacted by the heart attack."

Paddy nodded and went over to stand next to his uncle's bed.

"What's the risks?" he asked.

"Minimal. This is a very typical procedure," the older of the two doctors spoke.

"Typical to you, but not to us," Paddy said. "Please."

"Of course," he nodded. "The stent is a small wire mesh inserted into the blocked artery. If you would like to be awake you may, or we could completely sedate you. You will be asked to stay overnight if we do. We can use either the main artery in your wrist or your upper leg near the groin area."

Uncle Tully shifted uncomfortably, and Paddy had to suppress his grin.

"I'd prefer the wrist."

"Most men do," the female doctor chuckled.

"Either will need to be assessed. There would be no effect on the genitals," the lead doctor said. "After placement, you will be kept in for observation. As I mentioned if you chose to be fully sedated, you will be kept in overnight."

"All in all, how long will the procedure take?" Paddy asked.

"A little over an hour for the procedure but the recovery might make it closer to two hours before you can see him," the younger doctor said.

Paddy nodded slowly and resisted grasping his uncle's hand. The whole thing made him feel like a weakling.

"Now the question is, do you want to be awake?"

"Not particularly," Tully said.

"Then we'll send in the anesthesiologist. Lastly, if we have a choice, wrist or groin?"

"Wrist," Tully stated without hesitation.

"Somehow, I knew that would be your answer. We will begin prep. See you in there," the doctor said.

Once they left, Tully looked up at Paddy. "Pull up a chair, lad." Paddy did and took his uncle's hand when he offered it. "With any surgery, there's always risks, aye?" Paddy nodded, his stomach plummeting. "I need you to know a few things before I head in there, okay? I'm not expecting anything to happen and I expect to be around a long time. But... I spoke with Markus earlier. If the worst should happen, I already have everything set up so you get everything. I need you to step into my shoes and deal with the publishers. I'd also like it if you and Keera keep the house. But I'd understand if you would want to see it."

Paddy looked down, his breath coming in short pants. "Listen to me, lad," Tully placed a hand on Paddy's head. "I know you're worried. I know you're scared, but even though I don't expect anything to happen, it would be remiss of me not to tell you."

Paddy nodded but felt a tear leak out of his right eye. Uncle Tully wiped it away.

"I'll be fine."

"I lost my parents. Nobody wanted me. Then I had you. I... I can't lose you too, Uncle Tully. I can't. I'm not ready."

"It's a good thing I'm not going anywhere then," Tully winked. Paddy looked up at him as another tear slipped down his cheek. "Ah, come here, lad." Tully tugged on his hand and pulled him into a hug. "I love you."

"I love you too," Paddy muttered into his uncle's shoulder.

They pulled back and Tully cupped his nephew's cheek. Using the pad of his thumb, he wiped away the tear tracks. Holding each other's gazes for a long moment, they shared all their fears, hopes, and dreams. The connection between them so strong they could almost read each other's thoughts. But soon, a knock at the door drew their attention. A man stood, dressed in scrubs and a lab coat. Keera stood behind him.

"Mr. Jameson," the man began.

"Yes," Tully confirmed.

"Big fan of yours, sir. I'm the anesthesiologist. I understand you would like to be completely sedated during the procedure."

"Thank you and yes."

"Then, I have just a few questions for you before we get you prepped."

Since Tully opted to be sedated instead of a local anesthesia, his recovery time was extended. Two hours later, Paddy sat beside Keera. He had paced for the first forty-five minutes then sat next to her for the remaining time.

"How's Emmet?" he asked once.

"Ma says he's still not doing great. The doctor has told him he isn't allowed to work out and all he wants to do is get to the gym."

Paddy nodded slowly. "I get it. But he's better physically?"

"He had a checkup yesterday. So far he's healing well."

"And Mara?"

Keera looked away. "Apparently, Emmet went to Tom's and Chloe's house to see her, but she wouldn't talk to him. He was in such a state Tom had to escort him home."

"I hope she realizes what she's doing, and I hope they make up before Emmet loses all faith," Paddy said.

"Me too."

Keera took his hand in hers. Then movement near the

end of the hallway drew her attention.

"There he is," she said.

Paddy's eyes snapped to the gurney.

"Hey!" Tully's voice was heavily slurred, and his eyes were only half open. "Told you I'd be okay."

Paddy looked up at the attending nurse as she wheeled the bed into the room.

"He did well, no complications but he needs to sleep. He also will probably not remember any of this. I'll send in the doctor," she explained.

"She's so damned hot," Tully said a little too loudly as the nurse looked back and chuckled.

"How do you feel?" Paddy asked, seeing the bandage on his wrist.

"Fantastic," he answered exuberantly. "They didn't have to up my willie."

Keera giggled.

"Uncle Tully," Paddy disciplined.

"What? You have no idea how it would have been. I don't want anyone anywhere near *that* with a knife." Even Paddy chuckled at that. Tully yawned. "Damn, I'm tired."

"Sleep then," Paddy took the blanket and draped it over him.

"Oh!" Tully pulled up quickly and looked at Keera. "You! There's you! You, listen," Keera went closer to the bed. "I need to tell you something very important... You need to marry him. Yep," he raised his hands. "I said what I said."

"Okay that's all you get to say. Go to sleep," Paddy stated.

Tully blinked his eyes deliberately, then let out a giggle. Looking up at Paddy, he continued, "I'm drunk."

"No, you're high."

"Even better," he giggled again.

"Rest, Uncle Tully. I'll see you soon."

"Mm," he mumbled and closed his eyes.

Paddy sat in the chair to the right of Tully's bed and looked up at Keera.

"I'm sorry," he said softly.

"For what?" she asked.

"Not exactly how I was hoping to spend our weekend together."

"Hey," she breathed and walked over to him. Sliding down on his lap, she wrapped her arms around his neck. "I love you and I loved meeting your uncle. Yesterday was an amazing day in all ways," she winked. Paddy chuckled and wrapped his arms around her hips. Pulling her closer. He buried his head into her neck and took a deep breath.

"Thank you for being here," he said.

Running her fingers through his hair, she hummed. "Always."

Paddy pulled back and fused his lips to hers. The kiss felt almost desperate, like he was trying to keep one thing constant in his life. Before the kiss went any deeper, they broke apart and the doctor they had seen earlier, knocked on the door letting himself in.

Chapter

Twenty-Two

Keera poked her head into the hospital room after running down the hall to the restroom. Tully was still asleep, and Paddy sat on the small couch, eyes closed. His chest moved rhythmically up and down. He was asleep.

Finding another blanket, Keera shook it out and gently placed it over Paddy. Looking back at Tully, the small tray was near his left elbow, the manuscript resting on top. Biting her lip, she knew beyond a shadow of a doubt it was a bad idea. But she couldn't resist. Sneaking over, she took the papers and sat in Paddy's empty seat, beginning to read.

She just turned to the last chapter when she heard; "that

bad, huh?" Her eyes grew wide and they flashed up to Tully on the bed.

"Oh, my god, I'm so sorry. I didn't mean to—"

Tully raised a hand to stop her. "It's fine," he assured. "What did you think about it? Your brows furrowed a few times."

"How long have you watched me?"

"About fifteen minutes. My editor doesn't like it either. He says it's my worst one."

"No, I wouldn't say that."

"So, I've written worse?" He asked.

Keera chewed on her lip, "no," she acquiesced.

Tully chuckled. "It's all right, love. I have thick skin. I can take it. Tell me."

She huffed a sigh. "The thing is... What I love about you, is you can't be pigeonholed. You keep your readers guessing. I love that, but this? I'm sorry, but I figured it was the sister in the second chapter."

Tully winced. "Ouch."

"I don't mean any disrespect."

"None taken. What else?"

"Well... in three books you've had family members be the murderer. I just wonder..."

"What?"

"Are you perhaps using your own history with your family... Paddy's family, as inspiration? He told me about what happened after his parents died. I just can't help but wonder if maybe you're... rubber banding."

Tully was quiet for a long moment and Keera was certain he was angry with her. When he shifted in the bed and sighed, she pressed her lips together waiting.

"You're right," he finally said. She looked up at him questioningly. "I didn't realize it but you're absolutely right. I'm using my own anger against my family for what they put Paddy through. I didn't realize I was letting it affect my work. Thank you for making it known. So, having read it, what would you do differently?"

"Oh, I would never presume…"

"Presume away. I'm curious what would you change?"

Keera debated. "The title for one."

"What's wrong with the title?"

"Well… nothing," she said quickly. "It's just not…"

"Not what?"

"Not you. Not the book. *The Knife of Death* sounds more like a goth video game."

"What would you name it?" She looked down. "Tell me," he urged.

"I like the line your detective says. 'we're royally cooked'. I think it would be different and somewhat funny."

"A play on words."

"Exactly. The detective is a chef in a castle. It would pique my interest."

"Interesting. I'll consider it. What else?"

"The maid? What's her backstory? You make her mysterious and interesting and then nothing. Is she part of it? Is she, I don't know, a long last cousin of the royal family? She seems so much more interesting than a simple maid. Could she be the murderer? Or, did she see something? I just think the ending is forced. The clues worked oddly to make it to the sister."

Tully said nothing as he slowly nodded. "I like her, son. I like her a lot."

Keera spun around in her chair to see Paddy sitting up

on the couch behind her, wide awake.

"That's good, because I like her too," he smiled. Keera set the manuscript down and turned to him.

"The doctor said he wants to keep you overnight, but you can go home tomorrow," Paddy said. "I figured I could take Keera home and be back to get you." He looked over at Keera. "If that's all right with you?"

She nodded. "Sure, yeah."

"I'm sorry this happened during your weekend together," Tully said. "Not the most romantic time, I'm sure."

"No, it was wonderful meeting you, Tully and it was an amazing time reconnecting with Paddy," Keera said. "I hope we can meet again soon, and I hope you feel better. But I should get home. My cousin was just recently released from the hospital too."

"I hope he's feeling better," Tully said. "But you owe me a manuscript." She looked at him confused. "You read mine, not I get to read yours. It's only fair."

Keera swallowed and took out her phone. "Okay, I can email it to you."

"Paddy, you know I don't work well with those things. Print it out for me, would you?" Tully asked.

"Sure, Uncle Tully, on the way back."

Keera took a deep breath. It would be the first time anyone other than family read her work. She would be lying if she said she wasn't petrified but excitement also coursed through her veins.

Taking their leave of Tully, they left the hospital. Markus had offered to pack up their suitcases and check them out of the hotel, but after the long day, they extended their stay in order to go to the hotel, rest, shower, and change clothes, then get on the road.

Paddy pulled the car up to Keera's ma's house and put it in park. He cut the engine and turned to look at her, a soft smile lifting his lips.

"In a way," he began. "I have to say, though it wasn't exactly how I hoped to spend our time together, it was probably one of the best weekends I've ever had."

"Me too," she answered. "I loved meeting your uncle. Please keep me updated on him?"

"Of course."

"And I loved our time together. Sorry for going off the rails yesterday morning."

Paddy chuckled. "Forgiven and forgotten."

Keera leaned over the center console and kissed him. When they finally pulled back, Paddy stroked her face.

"I'll see you soon," he stated. "I want to get Uncle Tully home and settled, but I'll text you and call when I can."

She nodded. "No rush. If you can't talk, no need to tell me. I understand."

"God, I love you," he sighed leaning over and kissing her again.

"I would have you stay for as long as possible, but you should go back to your uncle."

"I have a manuscript to read to him," his eyes twinkled.

"Ugh, don't remind me," she laughed.

"I'm looking forward to it."

"Promise you won't laugh if you hate it?"

"Never," he swore. "I would never laugh at anything you do."

She bit her lip. "Do you think Tully is okay that I read his manuscript? I didn't mean to... I— it was there and–"

"He's fine. I've never seen him so interested in someone's opinion though. He likes you, Kee."

She smiled. "I like him too."

"I'll text you tonight?"

She nodded and got out of the car. Paddy walked her to her door. Another quick kiss and she walked inside, peeking out the side window to see him drive away.

"You home, love?" she heard her ma come down the hall.

"Yeah, ma," she replied turning to see Siobhan.

"Have fun?" her dancing brows made Keera laugh.

"So much," she walked over to her and embraced her.

"Good, I want to hear all about it. How was TS Jameson? Just as handsome as I expected?"

Sitting on the couch, Keera started telling Siobhan the story as her mom poured them some wine.

Chapter Twenty-Three

It had been a week. A solid week since Keera heard from Paddy, she had gotten a text from him telling her he had gotten back safely and was about to start reading to his uncle. But since then… nothing.

Immediately, she wondered if they both hated her book so much, they were hoping she'd forget she gave it to them to read. She sent a few texts over the week to Paddy, but they remained unanswered. She started at her phone. Her texts in blue but no grey replies. He had not sent anything since the first day.

Her mom bustled out of her room and into the living area adjusting her handbag strap. "I'm heading to Orin's and Deirdre's to check on Emmet. Do you want to come, love?"

"Yeah. Anything beats sitting around here waiting."

"Still no text?"

"No, I mean... I told him I understood but, come on. It would be nice for a little something. What if his uncle took a turn for the worse? Or what if something happened?"

"Oh, honey," Siobhan said. "I've been there, but all I can say is, it will be all right."

"How do you know?"

"That it will be all right?"

Keera nodded.

"Because there is nothing you can do to change it. Worrying yourself sick won't help you, Paddy, or his uncle. Trust me, love. Now, come on. Let's go check on Emmet."

Keera nodded. She knew her mom was right but she still worried. Grabbing her jacket, she followed Siobhan. Just as her mom opened the front door, she froze.

"Oh," Siobhan stated. "Patrick."

"Hiya, Ms. O'Quinn. Is Keera home?"

Keera looked around her mother to see Patrick O'Flannery standing on the stoop.

"We're just heading out, Patrick. You'll have to come by later," her mother said.

"No, Ma, it's okay," Keera moved around her mother and looked down at her ex-boyfriend on the steps. "What do you want, Patrick?"

"I just wanted to talk to you, Kee. I'm sorry about what happened the last time we met. I was jealous and upset. I never should have punched the man you were with. I wanted to say, I'm sorry and I hope you can forgive me."

"Yes, I forgive you, but we're not getting back together," she crossed her arms over her chest.

"No," his eyes grew wide. "No, no, I—I didn't mean for it to come across like that. I'm actually dating someone," he looked sheepish. "That's why I said we needed a break. I was seeing her too. I'm so sorry. I didn't know if it was going to get serious between us, but it has. She's actually pregnant."

"What?" Keera demanded.

"Yeah, it wasn't planned or anything, it just happened."

Keera took a deep breath. "Wow."

"Yeah, it was kinda sudden but I'm really happy. I always wanted kids. I know you didn't or don't. I couldn't imagine you being pregnant with my kid." He must have seen her mom step forward protectively, because he paled and put his hands up in a gesture of surrender. "Oh god, not that you'd be a bad mother. I think you'd be a hot mother, I just…"

"It's okay," Keera said and surprisingly it was. "I'm glad you're happy."

"Thanks, and are you? Happy, I mean. With that guy?"

"Yeah, I am. I'm really happy," Keera stated.

"Oh, good," he sighed. "I'm glad. Ehm… I have to go but maybe we could still be friends?"

Keera wanted to laugh but the look on his face stopped her. He was serious.

"No," she said. "I don't think that would be a good idea. We'll be friendly, but not friends."

"Okay," his smile faltered. After a beat, he took a step closer and kissed her cheek. "I really do like you, Keera. I'm glad you're so cool with this."

"I liked you too, Patrick. You'll be a fun dad."

"Thanks. I can't believe it, you know?" he sighed running his fingers through his dyed black hair.

"Trust me, I know exactly how you feel. Be well."

"You too," he smiled and turned to go. Once he drove

away, Siobhan placed her hands-on Keera's shoulders.

"Are you okay, honey?" she asked.

"Yeah," Keera nodded. "Let's go see Emmet."

Chapter Twenty-Four

Un-fricken-believable.

Paddy tried to quell his anger. He had never been so upset and he honestly didn't know why. He trusted Keera and it looked like a goodbye, but he wanted that boy out of her life for good. He didn't trust him at all. When he saw him kiss her cheek, Paddy's hand curled around the manuscript he held.

He watched as they got into Siobhan's car and drove off, but he couldn't bring himself to do anything more than stare after them. He had kept his communication with her at a minimum... nonexistent, really, over the last week, partly because he had a surprise for her and he was afraid he'd let it slip, but also because he was helping his uncle get more comfortable with the new chef he hired. Tully was on a strict diet and whiskey allowance.

Finally, Paddy was shaken out of his thoughts by his phone ringing a notification. Pulling out the device, he opened the text chain.

Keera: Miss you. Can't wait to see you again. I hope Tully is okay. Love you!

His hand shook as he stared at the text. He wanted so badly to text back and tell her he loved her, but he was just too upset. He never wanted to see that boy around Keera ever again.

Pocketing the phone, he headed back to his car, got in, and drove away.

Just as he pulled out of her drive, he saw the boy walking down the road, head down, typing on his phone. Paddy slowed, then parked the car. Leaving it running, he got out.

"Hey!" he shouted. The boy turned; his eyes grew wide as he recognized him. "You moving in on my woman, boy?"

"What?" he paled.

"You heard me," Paddy reached him by then and even though every fiber in his body wanted to throw a punch as payback for the sucker punch; his jaw still ached. "I saw you. I want you to stay away from Keera."

"I—I wasn't..." he stuttered.

"Then what the hell was that kiss?" Paddy demanded.

"I was saying goodbye." Paddy paused and the boy looked down. "I never loved her." Paddy growled. The boy backed up. "What I mean is, I cared about her, but I knew I was just a stand in for her."

"What are you talking about?" Paddy demanded.

The boy looked down and took a deep breath. "She always wanted you. I saw you that day over a year ago when Keera and I first met. I knew then I was just a stand in for you. And I was okay with that for a while but soon I wanted what she gave you... someone's heart. We took breaks but we always seemed to get back together. It was purely physical with us." His eyes darted around the deserted area. "But during one of our breaks, I met Sarah and... well, she's everything I wanted. We're together. She's actually pregnant. I'm going to be a da'. I couldn't have that with Keera. We don't care for each other like that."

Paddy held his tongue. He wasn't about to reveal anything. "You cheated on her?" Paddy spat.

The boy shook his head. "No!" he stated. "We were on break. But all I'm saying is, you don't have to worry about me. I'm not interested in her. She's all yours if she wants you."

"Of course she does," Paddy heatedly defended. "Just stay away from her. And no more kissing."

"I swear, no more, and... I'm... sorry. I'm sorry for punching you."

"I hardly felt anything," Paddy shrugged.

The boy's face grew red then he calmed.

"I'm trying to clean up my act."

"Good. Start by being faithful to the mother of your child, aye?" Paddy replied. "Any man can be a father, but only special ones get to be a dad." Uncle Tully's face flashed before his eyes. Paddy heaved a sigh. "Just stay away from her, and we'll be grand."

He headed back to his car and got in without another word to the boy.

"She loves you, you know. Always has," the boy called as Paddy put the car into gear. He paused a second but did not give the boy a reply. There was only one person who he would say that to.

Pulling back on the road, he didn't know where he was driving but soon, his uncle's house came into view.

He cut the engine and headed inside.

"Don't you even think about touching that," he heard Uncle Tully yell.

"Sir, you cannot have a secret stash."

"I don't have a secret stash, I tell you!"

"Then what is this?"

Uh-oh, Paddy thought. The chef had found the whiskey bottle hidden in the Buddha statue on the bookshelf.

"I don't know how that got there."

"Mmhmm."

"It's a miracle, I tell you. We should be grateful and accept."

There was no answer, at least not one Paddy could hear. He could guess though. The chef doubled as a live-in nurse and was there until the doctor had Tully do a stress test. Once he passed without any complications, the chef/nurse would be free to leave. But Paddy knew his uncle; for all his fluff and fuddle, he liked the company.

Following the voices to his uncle's study, the impressive amount of mahogany always took his breath away. He had memories in every room of the house but especially in the study. As a boy, he would sneak in to watch his uncle work. And many times, he would sit before his uncle, by the fire, to listen to him read his latest manuscript. As he got older, he would join Tully with a glass of whiskey beside the fire and they would talk about everything or nothing at all. It was his favorite thing to do.

Now, his uncle stood by the window, the chef long gone out the side door. Paddy took a second to observe his uncle. The setting sun shone down on him, casting him in shadow. Still taller than Paddy's six-foot frame, Uncle Tully always kept his back ramrod straight, a trait instilled in him by a military father. Though he teased the nurse in the hospital about exercising, he always looked after himself, and his physique was impressive. His salt and pepper hair still fell to his shoulders and his usual jeans, button up shirt and blazer made him look like he was about to go to a photoshoot for *Esquire* Magazine.

"I can feel your eyes on me, lad," Tully said, not turning

from the window. "And from the feel of tension in the room, something happened," he looked back at him. "Did she not like our plan?"

Paddy shook his head, huffed and buried his hands in his jean's pockets.

"I... I didn't talk to her," Paddy admitted.

Tully slowly turned fully around, his silhouette cast in shadow, making him even more imposing.

"And why not?" he asked calmly. Too calmly. When Paddy shrugged and kicked the toe of his boot into a gouge in the wooden floor, feeling like a surly teenager, Tully moved from the window and to his desk. Pulling open the drawer to his left, he dug and came back with a small bottle of whiskey. Paddy stared incredulously.

"You tell that fascist dictator about this, I will disown you," though he was serious, his voice held a teasing edge.

Paddy laughed outright as Tully poured a small glass for both of them. Walking over, after successfully hiding the bottle again, he handed Paddy one of the glasses.

After clinking glasses and taking a swallow, Tully closing his eyes at the flavor. Paddy sat on the dark leather sofa near the fireplace.

"I won't say anything so long as you pass on the one she'll pour for you later tonight."

"Ooh, you bastard," Tully chuckled. "One glass a night does not make me an alcoholic."

"No, but with the meds, you have to be careful."

"I know," he said. Tully looked more tired than usual. Dark circles rimmed his lids and even though it had only been a week, he looked as if he had lost a few pounds.

"What's wrong, Uncle Tully? Are you feeling all right?"

"I wish everyone would stop asking me that," he snapped and turned away from him. "I'm fine. I'm alive, dammit.

Just stop."

Paddy stared at his uncle's back as he huffed and stalked back to the window. Tully had never snapped at him. Something was clearly going on. Standing slowly, Paddy walked over to him. His uncle again huffed a sigh.

"I'm sorry, lad," Tully said. "You didn't deserve me snapping at you. You're only trying to help."

"What's going on?" Paddy asked.

Tully turned to look at him. They locked eyes and Tully cupped his nephew's jaw.

"Do you know how much you mean to me, Paddy?" Tully asked.

Paddy smiled slightly. "Yeah, you've always shown it to me."

"Good," when Tully said no more and sidestepped him to go to the desk, Paddy's brows furrowed.

"That's it?"

"What's it?" Tully replied.

"You're not going to tell me what's going on?"

"Nothing is going on. Now, why didn't you talk to our girl?"

"No, I'm sorry, Uncle Tully. I know there's more going on with you. I'm here. Talk to me."

"I'm fine."

"You keep saying that. I know it's not true."

"What do you want me to say?" He snapped again and pounded his fist on the desk. "Do you have any idea what it was like? Do you have any concept of what I went through? No, you don't, so why should I burden you with how I'm feeling?"

"It's no burden, Uncle Tully. I *want* to know. I need to know you're okay."

"For Christ's sake!" Tully shouted and threw the cut crystal whiskey glass toward the wall, shattering on impact. "No, okay? No, I'm not fine. I thought I was going to die. I was on the sidewalk and the most pain I have ever experienced gripped my chest and wouldn't let go. I fell to my knees and thought, that was it. I was going to die. I couldn't speak. I couldn't move. I don't even know who called emergency services. All I could think of was, this is it. And I couldn't tell you how much I... I love you and yet, I was so scared. I didn't want to die. I didn't want to leave you and I didn't... I didn't want to die." Tears gathered in Tully's eyes as he looked at his nephew. "So no, I'm not all right. I was faced with my mortality and all I want, is to go back to the way things were. I don't need the constant reminder. I can't even sleep. I worry I won't wake up and then where would we be?"

Paddy placed both hands on his uncle's shoulders and stared deeply into his eyes.

"You are alive and you aren't going anywhere." Hearing his uncle's worries made his own small upset over some stupid boy moving in on his girl a moot point. "But know this, Uncle Tully. I know you love me, my god everything you sacrificed for me throughout the last twenty years proves that. But you can't hide away, you can't bury yourself in work. You can't go back, and you can't move on until you work through how you're feeling. *You* taught me that. And yes, there will be some minor changes, but one thing that won't change is us. It never will."

Tully took a deep breath, closed his eyes, and nodded. Pulling his uncle into an embrace, he held him tightly.

Finally, they pulled back and Tully scrubbed a hand down his face.

"Ugh, well, should we check to make sure we both still have our balls?"

Paddy chuckled. "I still have mine, might want to check if you still have yours."

"Piss off," Tully grinned. "I've had mine a lot longer and know how to use the whole package."

"TMI," Paddy laughed.

"Speaking of your girl," Tully began.

"Didn't realize we were, but all right." Paddy moved back to the couch, took his whiskey, and downed the remaining liquid.

"What happened?"

Paddy shook his head. "Honestly, I just am an idiot."

"That's a given," Tully winked and, pulling out the bottle, poured another glass of whiskey.

Paddy cleared his throat and looked pointedly at the glass then his uncle. Tully went stone faced and growled, handing the glass to Paddy.

"So, what really happened?"

Tully sat in his chair at his desk and Paddy began telling his uncle about Keera and Patrick O'Flannery from the date they had to when he waited near the trees watching Patrick at Keera's house, and finishing with their conversation on the side of the road.

"Did *she* kiss *his* cheek?" Tully questioned and Paddy squirmed.

"No," he admitted.

"Did she show any indication she was remotely interested?"

"No," he said again.

"Did you text her about your conversation with the boy?"

"No," Paddy sighed. "I haven't texted her since I came back to the hospital."

"You… what?"

"I didn't want to accidentally give away the secret."

"Oh, Paddy," Tully shook his head. "What were you

thinking?" You already told me how she reacted when you left to get coffee. What do you expect will happen now? You slept with this woman and now you haven't talked to her in over a week? Have you completely lost your mind?"

Paddy knew he was right and pulled out his phone.

"No," Tully stopped him. "She deserves an *in-person* apology. Get your keys." Tully stood and locked up his desk.

"Where are you going?" Paddy asked.

"To make sure you don't screw this up."

Tully headed for the door, opened it, and waited for him.

"Get a move on, lad, neither of us are getting any younger," he made a sweeping gesture as if to say *after you.* "Get the car started. I have to talk to the dictator." He hooked his thumb toward the hallway leading to the kitchen. Paddy nodded, watched his uncle leave, and headed to the garage a plan forming in his mind.

Chapter Twenty-Five

Keera glanced at her phone for the sixth time in twenty minutes. The check up on Emmet had turned into a makeshift *get well soon* party as the family all arrived around the same time to *check up* on him. She and her mom had offered to help with anything Dierdre needed.

Trevor's grandparents had left for America the day before and Trevor stayed with Emmet, Orin, and Dierdre. Emmet looked better physically but his eyes were emptier than Keera had ever seen. He would not tell her what happened when he went to see Mara, but from the look on his face when she brought it up, she knew it didn't go well. Absently staring at him through the kitchen sink window as she washed some dishes, Keera jumped when Sean walked into the kitchen and smiled tiredly at her.

"How's fatherhood?" she asked grinning, seeing dark circles under his bloodshot eyes.

"Amazing," he replied. "Just a little tired." He held up his forefinger and thumb about an inch apart but slowly, teasingly, widened the distance apart. Keera laughed.

He opened the refrigerator and pulled out a bottled water and a beer. Popping the tab, he drank from the beer for a moment then sighed.

"I wouldn't give it up for anything, but I'm just tired. Fortunately, I don't have to worry about teaching right now, being summer break but I can't imagine how tired my wife feels."

Keera dried her hands and looked in the fridge, pulling out the white wine.

"A small glass for her?" she offered.

Sean debated then nodded. "She pumped earlier today and has enough milk to get through. Aye, she'd like that, cheers."

Keera wasn't surprised Ness went the breastfeeding route, but the whole *no alcohol* thing was tough for her to comprehend. Sean watched as she poured the wine and eventually leaned against the counter, folded his arms across his lean chest and asked, "so, you and Paddy O'Shea, huh?"

Keera froze for a moment, then recorked the bottle and put it away. "Yeah, you like him, right?"

He shrugged. "It's not important if *I* like him," he teased. "But yes, I do. He treats you well?"

Keera hesitated for a second, thinking about the unanswered texts but quickly nodded. "He does. And I love him."

"Good," Sean took the wine from her and, with a wink, he left to the back deck. *That was easy,* she thought and again, Keera checked her phone; nothing.

With a frustrated groan, she shoved it in her back pocket.

"What's wrong?" Emmet's voice came from the doorway. Keera looked up at him and forced a smile. He didn't need the added stress of her issues.

"Nothing," she said. "How are you?"

"The same as when you asked me ten minutes ago," he grumbled.

Keera had it with his grumbling, growling, and all-around irritable behavior. But instead of being upset with him, she simply walked right over to him and slid her arms around his waist. She hugged him, holding on even though he didn't hug her back. She angled her head so her ear was flush against this sternum. The steady rhythmic beats of his heart lulled her nerves. Her Emmet was alive and well.

Seeing Tully in the hospital a week ago, made her remember the horrible few days of not knowing if Emmet would make it or not. She missed him horribly. The old him. The one who would protect her, tease her, always be there for her. She wanted to take away all the pain, all the hurt, and help him find his way back or through, if back wasn't an option.

Then, a horrible thought occurred. What if his path led him to America? It was where his son's grandparents were. It was a fresh start without the memories of Mara.

The more Keera thought of it, the more it made sense and the more it hurt her heart.

"You're leaving, aren't you?" she questioned softly.

Emmet took a deep breath, her head rose and fell with the movement, then his arms came around her and he held her to him.

"I have to."

She nodded as tears slid down her cheeks. "When?"

"A few months yet," he said. "I already talked to Curtis about what's needed. He's talking to the US Immigration Office in Indianapolis to see what I need to do."

"Will you be gone forever?" she looked up at him.

His pained expression elicited a sob from her.

"I don't know, Kee," he replied.

"You'll come visit, right?" she begged.

"Yeah, maybe. But I'll keep in touch."

She nodded. She knew he was leaving, even figured it out, but it didn't help. "I will miss you so much."

"I know," his voice cracked. "I'll miss you too. But I can't stay here."

"I know," Keera hugged him tighter for a moment, not wanting to let go but then they heard the sound of little feet running toward them.

"Daddy!" Trevor called excitedly. "Look what I found!"

They turned to look and his little face, dirt smudged was so proud. He held up his hand and showed a small turtle.

"Can I keep him?" He begged.

Emmet smiled at his son and Keera was struck by how the cloudiness in his eyes dissipated when he looked at Trevor. He bent down to be eye level with him.

"That's amazing," Emmet praised. "Let's go look for more. Maybe, if you let him go, he'll show you where the rest of them are."

Trevor's eyes grew wide. "There's more?"

Emmet chuckled. "Possibly, let's go see." Emmet straightened and offered his hand. His son slipped his little one in his.

Keera applauded his skill in circumventing Trevor's desire to keep the small creature. The three of them headed out back to the sounds of laughter and the smells of food. At the threshold, Emmet looked back at her and pleaded.

"I haven't told anyone about..." he trailed off. "Please

don't say anything."

She nodded but her heart was still heavy. She watched as Emmet and Trevor stepped down off the deck and made their way through the yard to where Trevor had been digging.

Sinéad raced over to her, grabbed her hand and pulled her back into the house, through the kitchen, and down the hall to Sinéad's room. Shutting the door, Sinéad grabbed Keera's other hand and sat on the bed.

"So," Sinéad prompted.

"What?"

"So, I get a string of texts from you talking about going all DEFCON four on that bitch who hurt my brother, and then nothing. What happened?"

"You were here more than I," Keera replied. "What happened when Emmet went to see her?"

"I didn't go with him," Sinéad grumbled. "Idiot didn't want anyone with him. He snuck out. First thing we heard about it was when Tom knocked on the door and Da' opened it. Emmet was as white as a sheet. He stumbled up the steps and Da' shouted at us to call Cabhan. I called him while Ma talked with Tom. Da' got Em to his room and stayed with him until Cabhan got there. Meanwhile, Ma and I were talking with Tom. He said Emmet banged on the door, shouting for Mara. When Tom answered, he tried to push his way through, but Tom saw his eyes. He said he hadn't seen Emmet like that since..."

"Since when?"

"Since he was high on drugs years ago."

"You don't think..."

"No! I know Em is clean, but I wonder if maybe all the pills he's taking for the pain and whatnot might have caused him to relapse. But Tom said he was lucid and speaking clearly. He demanded to see his wife and when Tom told him she wasn't there, he called him a liar and again tried to push past him. Chloe came forward out of the kitchen and spoke to him. Tom said as soon as Chloe said she was so sorry for everything, Emmet fell to his knees and wept. Chloe wrapped him in her arms and he buried his head in her shoulder. Tom said it was hard to watch. Someone as strong as Emmet looking like a child wrapped in Chloe's arms. Tom got him a shot of whiskey and when he was finally able to drink it, he did. You know how their stairwell curves?"

Keera nodded.

"Well, apparently, Tom looked up as he rounded the bend with the whiskey. And he saw Mara sitting at the landing, silently weeping as she heard him. When she saw Tom had seen her, she hurried back into her room. That's when Tom helped Emmet up and got him home. He had stopped crying but he was like a zombie. I've never seen Emmet like that. It scared me."

"I'm sorry I wasn't here, love."

"No, no," Sinéad shook her head. "You were with your man. You have to tell me what happened there, too. But I just wish… I don't hate Mara now. I know she hurt him, but she's hurting too. She wouldn't be crying like that if she didn't truly care for him."

"Yeah, but then why not just come back to him?" Keera demanded.

"Well, what if she's scared this ex of hers has friends? He did say he would kill everything she loved. Maybe just maybe, she is trying to show there's nothing to hurt? If she separates herself from Emmet to protect him, and maybe Trevor too, she really does love him and it's killing them both."

Keera thought about what Emmet said to her. He was leaving. "She needs to come back soon then."

"She wouldn't probably until after the trial. She has to be sure he will not hurt anyone."

"She doesn't have much time."

"What?" Sinéad asked. "What do you mean?"

"Nothing."

"What do you know, Kee?"

"I know nothing. I just think that she is handling this extremely poorly and if she wants Emmet at all, she needs to talk to him. Quickly. Before he loses all hope."

"We can't say anything, Kee. Emmet doesn't want to talk about it, and he can't handle any more stress."

"I know," Keera groaned. "Ugh, god, this is so tough."

"Look, everything looks better after a glass of wine. Let's go and get some, aye? We can talk strategy later. She can't argue with both of us. If we go together and tell her we know why she doing this, maybe we can save a marriage and help my brother," Sinéad said.

"Deal," Keera answered. "Now, let's go before someone misses us and wonders where we are and why we're talking in secret." They got up and headed to the door.

"Yeah, oh by the way Cabhan and Racheal said Oisín took his first steps this week!" Sinéad revealed as they walked down the hall.

"Really? Gosh he's not even one! That's amazing. Are they thinking about having any more?"

"Oh, no," Sinéad laughed. "Racheal says four is enough."

"I get that. I couldn't imagine even one."

"You'd make a great mother," Sinéad said.

"You're the second person today to tell me that."

"Really? Who was the first?"

"It doesn't matter. Now, where's that wine?"

Keera and Sinéad walked out to the backyard and Siobhan offered her niece and daughter a glass of wine and poured them from the bottle in the ice bucket, then topped hers off. The three women said nothing, watching Emmet and listening to the conversations around them.

But in a moment, the hair on the back of her neck stood on end and she turned. Her Uncle Orin was unlatching the back gate, returning from a run to the off license, a brown bag in his hands, but it was who stood behind him that had her hands sweating and her heart racing.

Paddy.

He carried another brown bag and a medium giftbag in the other hand. He was smiling at something Uncle Orin had said but she saw the tightness around his lips and eyes. He may look jovial, but he was nervous. His eyes found hers and they turned worried.

"I told you it would be okay," Siobhan whispered.

Keera nodded and stared at Paddy, so relieved he was there. She didn't care why he hadn't responded to her. In that moment, all that mattered was he was there. Cabhan's eldest son; Lachlan, offered to take the liquor bags and headed inside. The thirteen-year-old looked the spitting image of his father, Keera's eldest cousin but soon Keera's attention was on Paddy again. The strained look was still in his eyes and as he walked up to stand directly before her, everyone quieted.

"Hiya," he breathed.

"Hey," she answered and threw her arms around his neck. "God, I missed you. Why haven't you texted me? How's Tully? Is he all right?"

"He's fine. I'm sorry I haven't texted. I – ehm – didn't think I could keep this a secret." He held up the giftbag.

"What's that?" she asked.

"Open it."

She passed her wine back to her mother and took the bag. Pulling out the decorative tissue paper, she saw a manuscript clipped by a large binder clip. She looked up at Paddy, her brows questioning. He said nothing, so she pulled it out and turned it over.

Royally Cooked

A Comedic Mystery

Written by: TS Jameson and Keera O'Quinn

O'Quinn was circled and two handwritten question marks were drawn nearby.

Her eyes widened and she looked up at him.

"What?" She breathed the question.

"Hold that thought," Paddy said. Looking back, he caught Orin's eyes, who nodded and opened the back gate again.

Uncle Tully walked around the corner and caught her eyes. He smiled then his eyes moved over her shoulder to her mom. His eyes widened then a very flirtatious smile lifted his lips. Tully walked up the deck and past Paddy.

"You must be Keera's sister," Tully offered his hand to Siobhan.

"Flirt, I'm her ma." Siobhan allowed him to kiss her hand.

"I call rubbish," Tully said. "There is no way you are old enough to have an adult daughter. Though, I see where Keera gets her beauty."

Paddy cleared his throat. "Uncle Tully?"

"Right," he winked at Siobhan. "To be continued..."

"I look forward to it."

Tully looked back at Keera who held the manuscript.

"So... what do you think of the title?" Tully asked.

Keera let out a nervous chuckle. "I love it... but what's my name doing there and why the question marks?"

"Well, it was your ideas that sparked my creativity. I have to say you were right about the maid. Very interesting character. I didn't give her the due she deserved in the first draft."

"Tully…" she breathed.

"Love, I've been in a writing slump for about seven months. We call it writer's block and you helped me. Both you and my editor were right. It was my worst work."

"I didn't—"

Tully held up a hand, "you were right. But with your help it has become one of my favorites. Even my editor praised it in its draft form… trust me, that's a rarity. When I read your manuscript, I was highly impressed."

"We both were," Paddy interjected.

"I spoke to Markus about you. He's interested in seeing your work, but I told him I needed your permission to share it with him. He's interested in representing you. Possibly helping you get published."

"Published?" Keera breathed. It was her dream, but she didn't think it would ever happen.

"What do you say?" Tully got down on a knee and winked. "Will you be my co-author?"

Keera giggled. "Yes!"

Tully let out an excited shout. "She said yes!" he teased. She hugged him as soon as he stood.

"Oh my god! I'm so excited! I can't believe it!"

Her mom hugged her nearly jumping up and down with excitement.

"Oh, and as for the why O'Quinn is circled, there's another gift in there, love," Tully motioned to the bag. Keera's brows questioned then she opened the bag back up. Looking at the bottom, there was a small package wrapped in white tissue.

She took the square item out and looked up at them both.

"Wait," Paddy stopped her. "First, I need to say I'm sorry."

"For what?" she questioned.

"I came by earlier today, but I didn't stay. I saw Patrick O'Flannery at your door. It pissed me off. Not with you," he hurriedly said. "But at the situation. At him. I left without talking to you."

"Paddy, he's in the past. He actually came by to say he was sorry for starting the fight."

"I know, we talked."

"You did?" She asked. He nodded.

She cupped his face making him look at her. "You have no reason to be jealous, angry, or upset. I don't want him. I want *you*."

"I want you too."

"Open the gift, love," Tully's voice was behind her. She hadn't seen him walk over to her mother.

At Paddy's nod, she unwrapped the small box. It was a jewelry box and her breath stuttered. Looking up at Paddy, he wasn't there. Her eyes tracked down. He knelt before her. She swallowed audibly.

"I love you, Keera O'Quinn. I never want to be parted from you. Whatever happens in this life, I want it to happen by your side. I knew from the very beginning you were the woman for me. I know we talked about this and I am not pressuring you at all for the other things we talked about. But I want to spend the rest of my life with you. Will you do me the absolute honor..." he took the box from her shaking fingers and opened it. The engagement ring glistened in the sunlight. "Of becoming my bride so we can journey together always?"

Tears blurred her vision as she looked from the sparkling ring to his hopeful eyes.

She looked over his shoulder to see her uncle. He smiled and nodded. Her eyes turned to her mother behind her, asking her approval. Siobhan wiped her tears and nodded, her smile, uncontainable. Keera's eyes fell on Emmet standing in the yard, his son's hand in his. His eyes contorted in pain for a brief moment then he nodded.

Finally, her eyes moved back to Paddy. Her worries of marriage, children, sharing her life and being forced to put her career on hold, vanished. The manuscript was proof of that. He would not demand she stop writing, he would support her, back her, and help her. He was her future. And she loved it.

"Yes, a thousand times, yes," she proclaimed.

Paddy let out a breath and then cheered. Pushing up, he pressed his lips to hers. The force of his kiss bowed her back. But he pulled away just as quickly and looked in her eyes.

"Are you sure?"

"Yes, absolutely. I love you."

Paddy whooped again and kissed her once more. Finally, when they pulled back, he slid the ring on her finger. It was a little big, but still fit.

"We'll get it sized," he promised.

"It's perfect," she stared.

"It was the first one I saw, and I fell in love with it."

"The salesperson didn't know what to do," Tully teased, still standing behind her with Siobhan. "Paddy didn't even ask, he simply said, 'that one' and 'I need it today'. Poor thing. It looked like the saleswoman was going to faint."

"You just bought it?" she looked at Paddy.

"After a not so subtle push from Uncle Tully, I realized what I wanted, and that's you."

"It's perfect."

They turned back to her family. Her mom, Aunt Dee, Ness, and her cousin's other wives were crying happy tears and cheering. Her cousins and Uncle were congratulating Paddy and meeting Tully.

Keera eyes looked for Emmet again, but when she saw Racheal, Cabhan's wife, holding Trevor, she knew he had left. Her one wish was for Emmet to be just as happy as she was, and she hoped it didn't take years for it to happen.

Epilogue

6 months later

"You'll call as soon as you land?" Siobhan asked. "And you'll let us know how everything is going? Please be careful, love and know if you ever want to come back, all our doors are always open for you."

Emmet nodded. "I know, Auntie. And I will let you know when I land. It's going to be pretty late here, but Curtis is picking us up." He looked down at his son, holding his hand.

Siobhan nodded and wiped her eyes. "Be careful."

"I will be," Emmet nodded. He turned to his father and Dierdre.

Dierdre dotted her eyes but it didn't help, her tears never stopped.

"Don't cry, ma," Emmet sacrificed his hold on Trevor's hand to embrace his stepmother.

"Oh, my boy," she sobbed into his shoulder. "Please, promise me you'll come home soon."

"I'll try, ma," he promised. Then, he turned to Keera as Dierdre crouched down to talk to Trevor.

"Thank you for waiting," Keera hugged him. "It wouldn't have been the same without you there."

"I'm glad to have been there," Emmet said. Then looked at Paddy. "Take care of her."

"I will," he promised and embraced him. "Thanks for being my best man."

"I was happy to do it," Emmet said. "Ehm..." he cleared his throat. "Come by some time? I'd love to see you both."

"We will, I promise," Keera said. Again, she hugged him. She always loved Emmet's hugs. In his embrace, she felt safe, secure, protected even. The only other embrace that felt like that was Paddy's.

"You'll find happiness again," Keera mumbled into his shoulder. "I know you will."

Emmet said nothing, only forced a tight smile.

A voice came over the loudspeaker saying Emmet's flight was boarding. Emmet looked at his family and took a deep breath, letting it out slowly. Taking his son's hand, he locked eyes with each of them, lingering a little longer on Ness's as she openly wept. They had a longer goodbye earlier, Ness begging him not to leave.

"Thank you all for understanding. I love every single one of you. We'll see you soon." He bent and picked Trevor up, anchoring him against his hip. Keera was happy to see he didn't grimace at the strain. He still hadn't been allowed to go back to his usual gym routine and Keera saw how the stress eating and extra beer had taken its toll on him. He still looked amazing, always had, but he had packed on about twenty pounds and for someone who prided themselves on their health and physical appearance, she knew it depressed him even more.

"We need to go," he looked over at her. "Text me pictures. I'm sure it's beautiful."

"We will," she promised. Paddy placed an arm around her shoulders and pulled her into his side, comforting.

"You ready, *mo leabh?*" Emmet asked Trevor.

"Yeah," he answered.

"Okay, say *bye bye*."

Trevor waved. "Bye, bye!" Then squealed as Emmet kissed his cheek.

"Let's go," he turned to go through the TSA checkpoint. Keera wasn't surprised when he didn't look back.

The family did nothing until he was through security and out of sight. As a whole, they sighed and turned to Keera and Paddy. The air shifted though only slightly, to happiness. Keera didn't mind, she was as sad as the rest to see Emmet go.

"Are you ready?" her mom asked, a twinkle in her eye as Tully wrapped his arm around her waist.

"I can't wait," she said. "St. Lucia, here we come!"

Everyone chuckled and it felt as if the spell was lifting. Paddy grabbed their carryon and shouldered her laptop case.

"No work unless absolutely necessary," Uncle Tully said, eyes poignantly on the computer.

"I won't. I promise," Keera said. "It's only for the flight and emergencies. Besides, Paddy already made me swear not to work more than an hour a day."

"Smart man, only measuring *work* as an hour," he winked at his nephew. "I'm sure as he is of my blood, *other* things will take much longer."

"Considering some of us women do all the work, I'm not surprised," Siobhan teased.

"Och, woman, you just wait until we're alone. I'll show you what happens when I'm in charge," Tully growled as he gripped her closer, his brows wiggling suggestively.

Keera giggled but loved seeing the sparkly diamond on

her mom's finger when she touched Tully's cheek as they kissed. She couldn't wait to go wedding dress shopping with her and planning the wedding for mid-winter. Keera was overflowing with ideas to make it the perfect fairytale wedding for her mom.

"We need to go," Paddy smiled. "We'll call when we land."

"Be careful," Siobhan called after them.

"Have fun!" other family members called as soon as they started walking.

"Oh shite, I forgot. Keera, Paddy, wait up." At Tully's voice, they stopped and looked at him. He jogged up to them. "So sorry. I forgot to give you this." He handed Keera a thin elongated box. "Open it."

Inside, lay a beautiful golden pen inscribed with her name on it. She gasped and looked up at him.

"My parents gave me a pen with my name on it for my first book signing. It's a bit early but... I heard back from Markus. As soon as you two are back, we are on our way on tour. Rest up. We have a busy next few months."

"Tour?"

"Book tour, love. Our *Royally Cooked* hit number one bestseller for three months in a row."

Keera's eyes sparkled. "A book tour? Oh my god. I can't wait!"

"Well, you'll have to," he winked. "Enjoy your honeymoon. I love you both. I know I'll be enjoying the house all to myself," he winked and looked back at Siobhan. Keera laughed and embraced him.

"Thank you, Uncle Tully."

"No, thank you, my dear, for listening to what I wrote in your copy of *Missing from the Collection*," he looked over at Paddy then back at her. "Thank you for not hurting him. Now, go, have fun."

Paddy and Keera embraced him, and she thanked her lucky stars she and Paddy gave each other a second chance. As she took her husband's hand and walked to their terminal, she smiled. Though Emmet was gone and he still hurt, her mother was engaged to a man who loved her fiercely, her best friend was married to the man of her dreams and they had a beautiful baby boy and Keera couldn't be happier to know she never gave up, followed her heart, and chased her dreams.

The next chapter of her life had just begun, and it promised to be a great one.

an deireadh

Acknowledgements

T hank you for reading! I am excited to share Keera's and Paddy's story! Ever since Keera was first introduced, I was curious to explore her past and I knew it had to involve *Playboy Paddy.* Their story was fascinating to write as it was not the quintessential love story but was much more real life. They have history, they each have a past, secrets, skeletons, but it was who they were together that they wanted to preserve.

It is a fitting end to *Love Among the Shamrocks Collection!* But never fear, a short story featuring Emmet O'Quinn is now available too! This features the time directly after he lands in America to his new life. And then look for the new collection; *Love Among the Shamrocks, the Next Generation* starting with book one *In Dublin Fair City* featuring a grownup Trevor O'Quinn and his love of musicals and one Cassandra Doyle. Then dive deep into the *Song of Heart's Desire* featuring Lachlan O'Quinn and his struggle after losing his wife ten years prior and how Corinne McDonnagh slowly breaks through his icy exterior. Finally, so far, fly across to Florida where Oisín O'Quinn, most sought after male model, tries to woo the stubborn Naomi Moon in *Chasing After Moonbeams!*

There's much more O'Quinn family to share!

Please visit my website for more books and information! www.mkatherineclark.net

Read on for *Love Among the Shamrocks Collection: The Next Generation, In Dublin Fair City.*

love among the shamrocks collection
the next generation

Book One

In Dublin Fair City

M. KATHERINE CLARK

Prologue

Trinity College Dublin

He looked around the opulent theater lobby seeing other guests in tuxes, ball gowns, and masks of varying styles. There were delicate masks, traditional black silk masks, doctor's masks from the time of the plague with their long noses and intricate designs, comedy-tragedy masks, colorful masks, masks that covered the entire face, the top half, or the side, animal masks, character masks, scary masks, elegant masks, anything one could think of, danced, mingled, and drank all around him.

He glanced down at his modern tuxedo. The jacket was fitted, a mark from his grandfather always telling him, a well-fitted suit told a lot about a man, and a white button up shirt, lined with a strip of black silk, and black round buttons. He had debated for nearly twenty minutes if he wanted to wear a tie, bowtie, or leave the top two buttons undone. Eventually, time was the determining factor and as he slipped on his black, red, and gold Venetian mask, he had tossed the strip of black that hung around his neck onto his bed and left his flat.

Standing in the Trinity College theater holding a glass of

whiskey, hearing the music, and seeing the dancers pair off, he dampened his nerves. The fifteen-foot Christmas tree stood off to the side near the bar decorated in gold, red, and green and of course their school colors of cool blue and steel grey lined the bar. The ivory walls were covered in ornate gold ormolus of vines, leaves, and pillar crowns. Beautiful statues of Greek gods looked down on him and he remembered how he felt the first time he stepped into the theater. It was breathtaking.

After a moment of admiration, he felt the hair on the back of his neck stand on end. Turning to the grand stair, he saw her. She stood at the top of the staircase, her off the shoulder sweetheart neckline red dress popped against the ivory-gold of the wall behind her. Her delicate Venetian swan mask gracefully covered the top part of her face, coming down to the middle of her nose, the left side fanned up like a swan's wing. She looked stunning, just the way he knew she would. Their eyes locked and he saw the flicker of surprise then the heat of a blush flushed her cheeks. But he caught no hint of recognition.

Good, all is going according to plan, he thought.

She started down the stairs, her eyes never leaving his. The side of his mouth ticked up as he saw the quick rise and fall of her chest and the flush coloring her neck. She stood two steps above him, but they were eye to eye, and she had yet to drop his gaze. It was now or never. Taking a deep breath, he channeled his father's deeper and heavily Irish accented voice to disguise his own.

"I've been waiting for you," he stated.

"Me?" she questioned.

"Aye," he replied, happy with his impersonation.

"Why? Do I know you?"

"Wouldn't you know me, if you did?"

"There's a lot of students here," she answered, and he smiled at her slight American accent. "Your mask is brilliant and covering most of your face. If I'm supposed to, I'm sorry," she shook her head, then her eyes narrowed. "There is something"

"Something?"

"Familiar... I feel like I do know you. What's your name? Take off the mask?" She reached up to remove it, but he gently caught her wrist stopping her.

He shook his head. "No, Cassie," he said. "You don't need to know me, yet."

"Please?"

"Dance with me," he offered.

She stared at him again for a long moment. "Why do I get the feeling my life will change depending on the answer?"

He said nothing, just placed his empty glass on the tray of a passing waiter and offered his hand to her. Cassie looked at the hand, then him.

"Please, tell me your name."

He thought a moment and when he heard the orchestral start playing *Music of the Night* from the *Phantom of the Opera*, he nodded.

"You can call me Phantom."

"Phantom?" she questioned with a grin. "That's not a name."

"It's enough of one," he replied. "Trust me."

"Trust is easy to come by, but a second chance rarely

happens."

He said nothing for a long moment waiting for her to slip her hand into his. She didn't hesitate. Walking over to the dancefloor, he took her hand and placed his other on the small of her back. In that moment, he was eternally grateful to his stepmother for teaching him how to dance.

The tempo was slow, and they danced together not speaking but never dropping each other's gazes.

"I've always cared for you, Cassie. I need you to know that. I suppose I am concerned about your reaction so that is why I do not tell you who I am. I don't mean to scare you or anything like that, but I have to tell you... I love you. I have for a couple years now. And aye, I'm not some stalker. You do know me. I even can claim the distinction of being a friend."

"I have several friends."

"I know," he answered. "That is why I am not being any more specific. Just know, if you need me, I'll always be there for you."

"How will I know how I feel if you don't tell me who you are? I could very easily be in love with you."

"Give me a task. Anything. I will do what you ask and come to you without the mask, only me and you can decide then if you want me or not."

Cassie stared into his eyes and just as the music climaxed, she nodded.

"Okay, Phantom," she smiled. "I have something I want you to get for me."

"Name it and it's yours."

Chapter One

Five Months Later

Trevor O'Quinn looked up and across the lawn toward the entrance to the Old Library of Trinity College in Dublin to see his half-brother and sister rushing over to him. There on a visit to see if it was where they wanted to go to school, Killian and Aoife laughed together before breathlessly coming to a stop in front of him.

Trevor smiled and closed the music book he was studying, stood from the park bench, and hugged his younger siblings.

"Well?" He asked. "How was it?"

"The tour was okay," Killian started, "But since I had already seen everything with da', it was somewhat boring."

"Same," Aoife replied. "But Uni guys are hot."

"Aoife," Trevor warned. "You're sixteen. You don't know what hot means... right?"

She just giggled at his overprotective brotherliness and continued. "I wish you could have joined us."

"I know, guys, I'm sorry. I had class," he explained. "But, hey, let's go across the way and get some coffee."

Aoife made a cute disgusted sound. "You know I don't drink that stuff. Icky black ink."

"Blame the American in me," Trevor winked. "I can't get enough of the stuff."

"Da' says we'll have to learn to love it when we go to University," Killian answered as they walked toward the archway exit to the little coffee shop near campus.

"Da' is right," Trevor replied. "When you spend all night studying and have an eight am class, trust me, coffee is a lifesaver."

Waiting until it was safe to cross the street, Trevor took a moment to watch his twin brother and sister and smiled. It had been seventeen years since he and his father Emmet and stepmom Mara had left America to go back to Ireland and though those first two years Trevor barely understood what was going on at his *Gaelscoil,* he was happy to be in his father's homeland. But soon, with his Uncle Sean's tutelage, he was able to excel and was accepted to one of the finest schools in the world, his father's *Alma Mater,* Trinity College in Dublin.

Since they moved back, his cousins both older and younger had been his best friends, at least until his twin younger brother and sister were born. Then he had the siblings he always wanted. They had been close ever since.

"Trev?" Aoife's voice cleared his mind and he focused on

his siblings standing on the other side of the road. He gave an awkward laugh and wave then hurriedly crossed the street.

"Sorry," he said. "My mind drifted."

"Everything okay?" Killian asked.

"Yeah sorry, honestly I was thinking about my first few years here in Ireland. It's nothing."

"We're definitely glad you, Mum, and Da' came back. I can't imagine growing up anywhere else," Aoife said.

"American isn't bad," Trevor replied.

"No, just, there's nothing like Ireland," she clarified.

"I'm right there with you," Trevor agreed.

They pushed the door open and stepped into the coffee shop. The smell of freshly ground coffee and chocolate assaulted their noses. Trevor took a deep breath and smiled, letting out a satisfied sound.

"My grampa always says there's nothing like the smell of fresh grounds," he said.

"No, thank you," Aoife teased. "I'll take a hot chocolate."

"One hot chocolate and a spiced orange cake, got it," he winked. "Can you get us a table?"

She nodded and with a thank you, she headed to a four topper by the window. Trevor and Killian stood together in line at the café.

"So, what do you think?" Trevor asked.

"What about?" Killian replied.

"About college? Have you told Mum and Dad what you told

me?"

Killian's eyes grew large as he glanced around to make sure no one heard him.

"Please," he started. "I told you that in confidence."

"I'm not going to say anything, but don't you think you need to tell them soon? You only have two more years until college. They should know before then."

Killian huffed a sigh and ran his hand through his dark brown hair, his ice blue eyes begged him.

"I don't know what to do," he admitted. "I feel like such a failure. Da' has so many plans. He wants me to do so much and I..."

"Hey," Trevor turned to face his brother. "Don't go there. You are your own person and our parents love you. They'll be okay."

"They'll not be very happy with my choice," he shrugged.

"Trust me, I know what that's like," Trevor clapped his brother on the shoulder. "I'll be with you, if you want. When you tell them."

His young face lit with hope. "Will you?"

"Of course! I'd be happy to," Trevor grinned. "I know how it can be to tell our parents something you think will change how they look at you but trust me, it won't. They love you."

"You know?"

"You remember the year I took off between final year and college? When I travelled with my grandparents?" At Killian's nod, he continued. "I was worried because da' did that too when he was my age and always regretted it. Said no matter how amazing his travels were, it threw the timing off. But when I told him, he was fine. Said it was my choice, my life to choose what I should do. He supported me."

"But you *went* to college… it's not the same," Killian grumbled.

"'Tis," Trevor stressed. "Anyway, enough about that. What do you want?" He indicated the menu hanging overhead. They were next in line and Killian studied the board. Once he told him and Trevor ordered, they waited for the drinks and took the number for the food. Meeting their sister at the table, she put her phone down and took her hot chocolate.

"Cheers, Trev," she leaned back in the wooden chair and took a sip.

"Careful, it'll be hot," Trevor cautioned.

"Scalding," she giggled and set it down, dabbing her eyes as tears formed.

"You all right?" he asked.

"Fine," she promised. "Just an idiot."

"We knew that," her twin winked.

"Lay off," Aoife laughed and took a glass of the ice water Trevor had ordered. "So, what were you guys talking about? It looked important."

Trevor didn't react but Killian's eyes grew wide and he looked at both of his siblings.

"Uh oh," Aoife leaned forward. "This looks fun. What happened?"

Aoife's large blue eyes danced; a finer point of her facial expressions learned directly from her mother; Mara. But the ice blue eyes were distinctly from their father, Emmet.

Trevor sighed and leaned back in his chair with his coffee. "If you really must know—"

"Oh, I must," she answered.

"I told Killian a secret," Trevor started.

"I like secrets," Aoife said.

"What I'm planning for my recital," he lied.

"Oh," she looked dejected. "That's it?"

"What do you mean, *that's it?*" Trevor chuckled. "It's a big deal."

"I was hoping for something a little more… juicy," she said.

"Juicy?" Trevor laughed. "So sorry to disappoint."

Aoife sighed and leaned back. "So, what are you planning? Final year recital is pretty big right?"

"'Tis," he answered as they accepted the two slices of cake he ordered from the barista. "Some talent scouts for master degree program usually come and it's my grade for several classes."

"How?" She asked digging into her favorite orange spiced cake.

"Not only singing but stage presence, aural skills, theory, and piano performance. They want to see it all. It's nerve-wracking. They throw shite at you just to see how you respond. One of my best friends last year was set to be best in his class and when they threw a choir back up and gave him a Mozart piece to sight read…" Trevor shook his head. "He ended up being about twentieth in his class. He warned me to be at the top of everything and be prepared for the most unexpected thing."

"Like a choir backup on a Mozart piece," Killian said. "From my limited knowledge, it's unusual. Normally Mozart is either choir or solo hardly any sort of mixing."

"You're right. Not unheard of obviously but not usual."

"So, what's this surprise you're cooking up?" his sister asked.

"I'm going to anticipate them and do something no one else has done."

"What's that?"

"You'll have to wait and see," he winked.

"No fair! You told our brother! What, is he your favorite?"

"I don't have favorites," he teased.

"So..."

Trevor looked at Killian. "Should I tell her?"

Killian shook his head, a devilish smirk on his lips. Trevor looked back at their sister and shrugged. Aoife kicked them under the table.

"Ow," Trevor bent down to rub his shin. "Damn, Aoife."

"That's what you get for not telling me," she pouted. After a second of both brothers laughing at her antics, she continued. "It's next weekend, right?"

"Saturday," Trevor nodded. "I'm ready just to get it over with."

"I bet," she said. "I don't think I could ever be a singer. The things you and Mum have to do? Getting out on stage in front of people?" she shuddered. "Scary."

"It can be," he shrugged. "But when it's something you love to do; it just makes it easy."

"Trevor?" a woman's voice called from behind him. He tried to prevent the instant smile that lifted his lips when he recognized the voice. Turning, he stood.

"Hey, Cassie," he greeted.

"Hey! How have you been? I swear I haven't seen you at all since we started this final session." she hugged him. He took a second to take a deep inhale of her perfume. She always smelled amazing. And that perfume meant something more to him. He remembered the one time he had searched high and low for it only to realize his main competition for Cassie's affections, Robbie McConaghy, heir apparent to his daddy's whiskey empire, had bought it for her and gave it to her first, successfully cutting him off.

Before he could reply, the said bastard, Robbie himself showed up and laid claim to her by an arm wrapped around her shoulders.

"There you are, baby," he said. Trevor caught her grimace.

"Yeah, hey," she answered. "I saw Trevor and wanted to say hello."

"Leave the Yank alone, you promised me lunch before our next class and I'm looking forward to dessert," he licked the shell of her ear, his eyes on Trevor.

The message was clear, *back off.*

Cassie forced a smile. "I'll see you later, Trev?" she asked.

"Yeah sure," he answered. Robbie gave him his trademarked smarmy smile saying *not going to happen.* Trevor watched them go.

Having meet Cassie his first year at Trinity, they latched on to each other when they learned their mothers were American and Trevor had yet to fully adopt an Irish accent from having lived the first few years of his life in America. Cassie's accent was subtle since she was born in Ireland but had an American accent at home while she was growing up. Sometimes she used Americanisms only Trevor and the other small handful of undergraduates from America understood. Their friendship grew over the last three years until Robbie wheedled his way in between them.

Watching them leave the café, Trevor huffed a sigh and turned back to his siblings.

"What was that?" Aoife asked.

"Hmm? Oh, um, a friend. Cassie," he sat down.

"Not her, the wanker," Aoife said.

"Aoife," Trevor scolded. "Mum will blame me if she hears you speaking like that."

"Tosh, ma knows it's da' not you. Besides, if ever there was an appropriate use for that term, it would be him."

"I agree, Trev," Killian said. "He basically licked her, claiming she was his."

"Well, they've been dating since Christmas so I would assume she is his," Trevor replied taking a drink of his coffee.

"A woman doesn't belong to a man," Aoife stated.

"That's not what I mean, Aoife and I agree with you," he said.

Aoife paused, looking over her now cooled hot chocolate, observing her brother.

"You like her," she deduced.

Trevor paused. It was on the tip of his tongue to deny it but he swore he would always be truthful with them so they would always feel comfortable coming to him with anything. Taking a deep breath, he let it out slowly.

"Aye, Aoife, I like her a lot."

"Then why do you allow him to treat her that way?"

"It's not my choice, nor is it my job to protect her. She's dating him. She chose him. There's nothing I can do."

"Bollocks," Killian replied. "You always taught me to fight for what I want. Hell, da' tells us all the time… literally… all… the… time how he had to fight for Mum. How would he feel if he knew his eldest son wasn't fighting for something he loves and wants?"

"I don't love her," Trevor defended.

"Maybe," Aoife said.

"Poor use of words," Killian replied at the same time. "What I mean is, you like her, and *he* clearly thinks of her as a possession."

"She likes you too," Aoife interjected.

"And she likes you too," Killian acquiesced. "You should give it a try."

"Leave it to my *younger* siblings to tell me what I should do with a woman," Trevor shook his head.

"We're not telling you anything Da' hasn't said before," Aoife laughed.

Killian's and Aoife's phones buzzed at the same time making them jump.

"Shite," Aoife cursed. "We got to go. The next tour is

starting in ten."

Trevor drained his mug and set it on the tray. "Let's go then."

"You don't have to walk us across the street, Trev. We're fine. Finish the coffee in the carafe. We'll see you at dinner. You're still able to meet us for dinner, right?"

"Absolutely, I'll meet you at the pub across from my flat. My last class ends at four-thirty. The tour should be over around that time."

"We have a Q&A from four-thirty 'til five so we might be late, but we'll see you around then!" Aoife threw the last few words over her shoulder as she and Killian rushed out of the café.

Trevor chuckled remembering when he went on his first college visit to a different college in Galway where his cousin Fiona was studying technology and computer science. The tour guides were sticklers for punctuality.

Pouring the last of the coffee in his mug, he hummed a song, one in his repertoire the judges might ask for and pulled out his theory prep book. Turning to the last page of the notes section, he added another little idea to his list for the recital. He wanted to surprise the judges. Knowing everyone else would be reactive to what they said, he wanted to be proactive. Maybe it was the American in him but whatever it was, he enjoyed toying with a few ideas on how to beat them at their own game.

Chapter Two

The next day flew by as everyone on campus was getting ready for their final exams and the music school worked on their juried finals. With everything piling up, Trevor hadn't had a chance to call his dad for a couple days. Something he did every evening and as he fell into bed after midnight, he pulled out his phone and clicked over to his dad's text chain.

For the first few years of his life, Emmet O'Quinn had been a larger than life unattainable entity but when his mother died, his father moved with him to America. To this day, Trevor could not remember his mother, but he missed her more than he thought possible. Those four years he and his father spent together in America were an elusive memory, but it built the foundation of their relationship. His dad became more than a dad, he was his best friend and confidant. They moved back to Ireland and Emmet and Trevor's stepmother Mara renewed their vows, but Emmet made sure Trevor was still his number one priority.

When Mara's band *Celtic Spirit* went on tour, it was only Emmet and Trevor again for a short time. But when he was on summer break, Emmet would pack Trevor up and they would meet Mara on the road in America, Australia, France, Germany, Italy, wherever she was touring, and those memories made him smile.

The birth of his twin siblings, Killian and Aoife had put an end to their travels for a time. When they were born Mara took a break from singing for three years, then went on a comeback tour but by then, Trevor was twelve and able to help his father be a stay-at-home dad. When Mara's album went platinum, Emmet took less and less time at the dealership he owned. Soon, he sold it to Trevor's Uncles Paddy and Tom, Keera's and Chloe's husbands.

It was Mara who inspired Trevor to pursue his own singing career and even had him in the studio with her occasionally. Mara always treated him as her own son even though Trevor's mother, Jennifer had died when he was two.

When one of Mara's songs came over his headphones, he smiled but as her hauntingly beautiful voice sang *Raglan Road*, tears gathered in his eyes.

This was the time of year he hated the most. He hadn't been back home to Kerry since the new year and he missed his family. All of them. Two dozen cousins, his aunts and uncles, his Grandma Dee, and Grandad Orin. He missed his Aunt Charlotte and Uncle Derek and his cousin Peter back in America and especially his gramma and grampa, his mother's parents.

He missed his old dog too. His dad had kept the promise me made to get him a dog and took him to the pound to pick out his new pet. The memory of the old slobbery face of his lab-terrier mix crossed his mind and as sad as it was to lose him three years ago, he was so happy to have the sweet memories. Emmet had buried him next to his old lab, Jacks in his grandparent's backyard.

His throat closed with emotion. Letting out an irritated grunt, Trevor wiped his tears away and turned back to his text chain with his father.

Trevor: Hey, dad, sorry I've been MIA for a couple days and couldn't call you back. I hope everything is okay. I know you would have left a message if it wasn't. Miss you and Mum. Miss talking to you but with final exams and jury coming up, my life has been eat, sleep and study... though seeing the time it's more eat and study, than sleep. Anyway, miss you, hope to talk to you soon. No need to call or text back, I know you're probably asleep. Love you. Night.

Almost before Trevor set his phone down to charge, his dad's face popped up on the screen along with his special ringtone. Trevor smiled and answered the video call. His father's face filled the screen, his ice blue eyes and red hair, so similar to Trevor's, he grinned.

"Hiya, dad."

"Oh, Trev, it's good to see you, son. How are you? How's things? How's school?" Emmet asked.

"Good, yeah, busy. Did I wake you?" Trevor asked trying to ignore how much he wanted one of his dad's hugs telling him everything would be all right.

"Nah, I was up. Watching a scary movie with your mum who fell asleep on me, so now I'm checking every door and window to make sure it's locked."

Trevor chuckled. "It's the Irish countryside, dad. What evil monsters could be lurking there?"

"Aye, well, you'll never guess where this movie took place."

"The Irish Countryside?" he guessed.

"Aye," Emmet chuckled then paused near the dining room window and turned his full attention on his son. "You doing all right, lad?"

Trevor nodded. "Just miss you."

"I miss you too, but I'll be seeing you on Saturday."

"Can't wait."

"How's things, though? Killian said he and Aoife had a great time visiting you and Trinity. It would be nice to have all my children go there."

Trevor debated but decided it was best. "You know, dad…" he started. "You might want to think of other options for them."

"Other options? Like what?"

"Like the possibility one or both may not want to go to college."

Emmet was quiet and Trevor kicked himself seeing understanding in his father's eyes. He should never have said anything. His brother may never forgive him.

"I wondered why he went. Your mother and I both know he doesn't want to go and hasn't told us yet. I'm glad he confided in you. I just hate the idea he won't get a degree. In today's job market an undergraduate degree is required for most good paying jobs."

"What do you mean?" Trevor questioned.

"Mara and I have known for a while Killian was looking at alternatives instead of university. We haven't said anything to him, hoping he would come to us himself, but he hasn't yet."

"Maybe mention in passing that it's all right not to go? That you wouldn't be disappointed in him," Trevor offered.

"I could never be disappointed in any of my children. Does he honestly think that?"

"I know nothing," Trevor replied. "I've already said too much."

"Of course," Emmet agreed. "I'm glad he knows he can confide in you. I'll say nothing about you mentioning it to me."

"Only because I worry about him."

"We both do, he's sixteen, you remember how it was back then."

"God, do I ever," Trevor chuckled. "It was brutal."

"It was for me too, yeah," Emmet replied. "Sixteen was… difficult."

They were silent a moment just staring at each other until Emmet cleared his throat. "So, are you ready for your jury Saturday?"

"I think so, yeah. Though as mum says you're never completely ready and that's okay."

"She definitely says that, so she does," Emmet answered. "Have you given any more thought to grad school?"

Trevor had brought it up at Christmas recess and had been met with encouragement but the more he thought about and researched it, the more school in America appealed to him. But the thought of leaving his family for a solid two years made his heart hurt. He didn't know how his dad had been able to leave Ireland for a midsized big city in the heartland of Middle America for three and a half years when Trevor was a child before Mara came back into their lives.

"I have but I'm not sure."

"Why's that?" Emmet asked.

"Well, for one it's expensive and two I don't know if I could be away from you all for that long."

"Don't worry about the money. Your mother left you that college fund and over the years I've been fortunate enough to add to it. You're set for grad school, if you want."

"It's not that, dad," he answered. "Not only."

"Being away from us?" he questioned.

Trevor nodded. "Yeah, I miss you guys so much right now and I'm only four hours away here."

"You've been away before. That time you went to stay with your Aunt Charlotte and Uncle Derek while your mum and I went on her comeback tour."

"I was twelve, it was an adventure," Trevor justified.

"Okay," Emmet chuckled. "Well, then the time you went travelling with your grandparents."

"I know but I had them with me. If I go to grad school in America, I'll be alone for two to three years."

Emmet was quiet for a long moment, but his eyes gave him away. "America?" His voice was tight.

Trevor clamped his mouth shut. He hadn't meant to let it slip.

"You're looking at grad schools in America?" Emmet clarified.

Taking a fortifying breath, Trevor plowed ahead.

"Yeah," he admitted. "I am. They're the best schools for opera besides Italy, of course. And as a citizen, it's easier to get in. I haven't done anything," he hurried. "I've only looked."

Emmet cleared his throat softly. "Well, Trev if that's your desire, I back you. I'll miss you. But I back you. I would never want to stand in the way of your dreams."

"I know that. I just don't think I could be on my own that far away... never mind, you know what? My dad never taught me to be scared. He always taught me to follow my dreams and that's what I need to do."

A wide grin spread across Emmet's face. "That's my lad," he stated. "But now, tell me, any news on the other finals? How's studying going?"

Talking to his dad until well past one in the morning, Trevor signed off with a *talk soon* and *I love you*. Placing his phone on the nightstand, he pulled off his t-shirt and sweatpants. Flopping down onto the mattress in his boxers, he turned on the television and turned off the light.